Return to
Broken Crossing

Also by Lee Hoffman
in Large Print:

Bred to Kill
The Valdez Horses
Wiley's Move

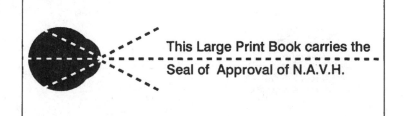

Return to Broken Crossing

LEE HOFFMAN

 WHEELER
PUBLISHING

Published in 2005 by arrangement with
Golden West Literary Agency.

Wheeler Large Print Western.

The text of this Large Print edition is unabridged.
Other aspects of the book may vary from the original edition.

Set in 16 pt. Plantin by Elena Picard.

Printed in the United States on permanent paper.

Library of Congress Cataloging-in-Publication Data

Hoffman, Lee, 1932–
    Return to Broken Crossing / by Lee Hoffman.
        p. cm. — (Wheeler Publishing large print westerns)
    ISBN 1-59722-077-9 (lg. print : sc : alk. paper)
    1. Large type books. I. Title. II. Wheeler large print
western series.
    PS3558.O346R48 2005
    813'.54—dc22   2005016142

Return to Broken Crossing

As the Founder/CEO of NAVH, the only national health agency solely devoted to those who, although not totally blind, have an eye disease which could lead to serious visual impairment, I am pleased to recognize Thorndike Press* as one of the leading publishers in the large print field.

Founded in 1954 in San Francisco to prepare large print textbooks for partially seeing children, NAVH became the pioneer and standard setting agency in the preparation of large type.

Today, those publishers who meet our standards carry the prestigious "Seal of Approval" indicating high quality large print. We are delighted that Thorndike Press is one of the publishers whose titles meet these standards. We are also pleased to recognize the significant contribution Thorndike Press is making in this important and growing field.

Lorraine H. Marchi, L.H.D.
Founder/CEO
NAVH

* Thorndike Press encompasses the following imprints: Thorndike, Wheeler, Walker and Large Print Press.

Chapter 1

"You in town for the hanging?" the short man asked. His dark sly eyes were on the stranger but his words seemed aimed at the bartender. And they seemed to hit him hard, as if they touched a point already galled raw.

"No, just passing through. Didn't even know there was gonna be a hanging." The stranger picked up his beer and drank from it, studying Shorty over the rim.

"He ain't been convicted yet," the bartender grunted.

Shorty grinned. His lips peeled back over his teeth like a wolf's. "He will be. Don't you fret none about that."

The beer was good even if it wasn't cold enough. It cut through the dry dust in the stranger's throat. He swallowed slowly, glancing from one man to the other. What was between them was none of his business, he figured. But it did stir a mild curiosity in him. Putting down the mug, he wiped at his mouth with the back of his hand, then asked, "They got a guest of honor lined up for the party?"

Shorty's grin broadened. "They sure have. Got him in the jailhouse now. Feller by the name of Shea Glencannon."

Frowning slightly, the stranger looked at his own reflection in the backbar mirror. It was, he thought, a fairly ordinary sort of face. Road dust smeared it now, dunning the lank black hair and a week's worth of scrub whiskers. But even so it was the same face that always gazed back at him from mirrors. He raised an eyebrow quizzically and the image did the same.

Shorty's eyes followed his, touching the reflection. "You look like you've done some hard traveling. Maybe you'd be interested in a fresh mount? I got a couple of good head of saddle stock I'm looking to trade."

The bartender grunted scornfully.

"Good stock," Shorty repeated. "I wouldn't consider trading except I need some cash. Either of 'em would be worth a good boot on a trade. Sound solid animals with lots of bottom. Perfect for a man doing hard traveling."

"I got a good horse," the stranger said abstractly, still gazing into the mirror.

"What about a saddle gun?" Shorty suggested. "I've got a new model Winchester that might come in handy for a traveler. I could make you a good price on it."

"I got a good horse," the stranger said again, as if he hadn't quite been listening. "Brought me here from Arizona. Reckon he'll get me wherever I'm going."

"Arizona, eh?" Shorty threw a sharp-edged glance at the bartender's broad back. He was talking toward the stranger, but pitching his words at the barkeep again. "You come from down there, eh? Ever been in a town called Gwinnett?"

The stranger's attention jerked away from the mirror. Expressionlessly, he answered, "I might have been."

Shorty had a hen-house grin smeared all over his face. He said vigorously, "Then you must have heard of this Shea Glencannon. Folks have been saying he's made a real mean name for himself raising hell in Arizona. If ever there was a man deserved to have his neck stretched . . . you must have heard of him."

"Yeah," the stranger muttered, vaguely amused and more than mildly curious. "But what are they hanging him *here* for?"

"Murder!" Shorty waved his arms like a playactor. "Just about the vilest, lowest-

9

down kind of murder a man ever —"

A crash of glass shattered across his words.

The stranger's head jerked. He saw the bartender bending to gather up the shards of the mug he'd dropped.

"Ox." Shorty grinned, pleased at the reaction he'd provoked.

The stranger unwrapped his fingers from the butt of his revolver. He pressed his hand against his pantsleg, wiping dampness from his palm. Turning his attention to Shorty again, he started to speak. But the little man was quicker of tongue.

"Ever see the like of this?" Shorty fumbled in a vest pocket. Bringing out a massive gold watch, he dangled it at the end of its chain. He shaped his face into a sad pained expression. "I hate to part with it, but I'm kinda hard up for money."

The little man seemed like he'd bust apart if he didn't manage to make a sale of some kind, the stranger thought. He wondered if it was desperation for money, or just that urge to trade that some folks have. From his slick dress and the iron he sported, Shorty didn't look hard up.

Casually, the stranger took the watch and examined it. Right handsome timepiece. Probably kept railroad time. He turned it over, admiring the fancy engraving on the case. "How much?"

"Listen to this," Shorty snatched it back and pressed a stud on the case. The big pocket piece made small bell-chimes somewhere within itself. "Ever seen the likes of it?"

It had played a piece of a tune. That intrigued the stranger. "How's it work?"

"Just push this thingamabob." Shorty touched the stud.

The stranger nodded. "I mean what's it got inside to make it do that?"

"Hell, I don't know!" Shorty seemed annoyed by the question. "Look, it's worth a hundred easy. I'll let you have it for sixty."

The stranger considered. He sure did wonder how it made that music. Thing like that would make a real fine present. And if it turned out there was no one left to give a present to, he wouldn't mind keeping it for himself. Slaunchwise, he watched Shorty fidget for a moment. "I might could give you thirty."

"I couldn't hardly let it go for less'n fifty!"

The stranger worked a hand into a pocket. He brought it up full of coins and picked out a couple. He was aware of Shorty's eyes on them like a wolf's on a new foal. The little man didn't *need* money, he thought. He *lusted* for it.

Shoving the rest back into his pocket, he held out four shiny eagles.

Shorty studied over them as if he were trying to pluck those old bald chickens with his eyes. He had the look of a gambler fevered with the urge to win. At last he sighed. "Forty."

Holding back a grin, the stranger took the watch. Then he glanced at himself in the mirror again. "This feller they're going to hang — this Shea Glencannon — you say he's in the jail right now?"

Shorty nodded, still gazing lovingly at the money he held. He looked up as the stranger turned toward the door, and called, "Pleasure doing business with you."

Stuffing the newly-acquired timepiece into a pocket, Shea Glencannon paused outside the saloon. He stood squinting against the brightness of the sun, looking for the jailhouse. He was real curious to have a look at this man the town was planning to hang.

A weatherworn sign across the street and down a ways read TOWN MARSHAL. Glencannon strode toward it.

The town of Broken Crossing had sure changed in — what was it? — nigh fifteen years, he thought. Saloons, hotels, a café, stores and houses. People on the plank walks and buggies on the streets. Pretty nigh a city now. The last time he'd seen it, it hadn't been anything but a few scattered cabins and a trading post.

The marshal's office was a squat, solid structure of roughhewn timber with the same heavy-browed forboding look that jailhouses seemed to have all the way from Galveston to Boise City. It had one big glass window, but the glass was painted over up past eye-level. Another window didn't reach down to eye-level. And there was no glass in it. Just bars.

He pulled off his hat and slapped it against his thigh, sending puffs of dust from both the hat and his pantsleg. It had been a long, hard trip. Especially the last few days — after he'd discovered that he was being followed. Settling the hat square on his head, he pushed open the door and walked into the marshal's office.

There were no lamps lit. The light that managed to get through the film of dust on the unpainted panes of the window gave the room a musty twilight look. The walls were bare, the low rafters unpainted, stained dark with time and lamp smoke. There was a solid wall between the office and the cells, with a heavy oak door set into it. Walking into the office felt a little like walking into a coffin — an old, used one.

Glencannon paused and looked at the man leaning back in the swivel chair. His chin was on his chest and his boots crossed on the paper-littered desk. It was Ted Edwards. Fifteen years' worth of growing from a boy to a man had changed his face but the features, the long, straight nose, the wide jaw, the almost colorless hair and brows, were the same as Glencannon remembered them. The star pinned on his shirt said that Edwards was town marshal now.

Grinning to himself, Glencannon shook the sleeping lawman's shoulder.

Edwards groaned.

Glencannon shook a little harder. Finally Edwards forced his eyes open. It seemed to take a lot of effort.

Touching his fingertips to the brim of his hat, Glencannon said, "Howdy, Ted."

Edwards blinked sleepily and looked at him. In the vague light, the marshal's pale blue eyes were blank. He squinted, then frowned in disbelief. Tentatively he asked, "Shea?"

Glencannon nodded.

14

Edwards shook his head as if to deny it. Screwing his eyes shut, he knuckled them. He opened them again and stared. "But you — you're — you're Shea!"

Glencannon nodded again.

Edwards shook his head again. He started to rise but didn't quite make it. Slumping back into the chair, he looked toward the oak door. "Then who's that? What's going on here?"

Shrugging, Glencannon said, "That's what I wanted to ask you."

"I dunno. I'm kinda confused. I —" Edwards hesitated, his face twisted into a deep frown. "He said he was you. So did your pa. I dunno. My head hurts something awful. You think maybe I'm still asleep?"

"Nope." Glencannon settled himself on the edge of the desk. "My own pa said this feller was me?"

The marshal nodded.

Studying on it, Glencannon told himself that maybe after fifteen years an old man could take a stranger to be his own son. But he didn't like the idea. It hurt his pride to accept it. He asked, "What would somebody else want to be me for? Especially if it's a hanging offense?"

"I dunno." Edwards pressed his hands to his temples. "I can't think straight. Not

15

with this pain in my head. *I* thought he was you. I was afraid I was gonna have to hang you."

"Would you have done that, Ted? Hung an old friend like me?"

"I dunno. You sure ain't been acting very friendly. All the time you — him — all the time he's been here, he's shied away from me. I figured it was on account of I'm a lawman now and he — you — with the reputation you got yourself since you left home —"

Glencannon grimaced slightly. But he knew the name he'd been acquiring. He couldn't blame Ted for such notions.

"Your pa said he was you," Edwards repeated, rubbing his head again. "I feel awful. You got any notion what time it is, Shea?"

Pulling out the new timepiece, Glencannon snapped it open with a flourish. "Close onto noon."

"Fancy turnip. You been doing right well?"

"Just bought it over at the Grand Oriental Palace saloon." He pressed the stud that made its musical innards play.

"You've been to the Oriental already? Then you know . . . ." Edwards' voice was still hazy. He squinted thoughtfully.

16

"Noon? I musta slept straight through the night. You reckon maybe I'm sick or something? I got a deputy that's laid up with the measles right now."

"You ain't got spots on your face," Glencannon told him. "How about you let me take a look at this other Shea Glencannon?"

Edwards fished a key ring out of the desk and got to his feet. Unlocking the heavy oak door, he shoved it open and stepped through. He stopped so suddenly that Glencannon almost walked into him.

Following his fixed gaze, Glencannon saw the thing on the floor of the back cell. It was the body of a man.

Edwards fumbled with the keys. He got the barrel door open and stepped in to kneel beside the body. When he looked up his face was chalky white.

Softly, emotionlessly, Glencannon said, "Shotgun."

Edwards nodded agreement.

"From up real close." Glencannon glanced toward the small barred window that overlooked the backyard. It was well above eye-level. He speculated. "Through that."

Again, Edwards nodded wordlessly.

"Caught it full in the face." Glencannon's voice was calm and cold, but his thoughts raced wildly. Hunkering, he picked up the limp right hand. The palm was smooth, the nails trimmed almost to the quick. There were calluses, but only on the tips of the fingers.

"No rope scars," he muttered as he dropped it and picked up the other hand. The nails were longer, neatly trimmed and almost clean. The skin on the thumb and the first two fingers was thickened but not really callused. No real calluses at all. He couldn't figure what a man with hands like that might have done for a living. Letting the hand fall, he asked, "Did he really look like me?"

"Kinda. Close onto being your height, I think. Heavier set."

"What was his face like? When he had one."

"Like yours," Edwards said, studying him. "Ordinary sort of face. Wore moustaches and a full beard, covered most of his face. But his eyes were an awful lot like yours."

Glencannon looked at the dead man's boots. Flatheeled. Faint scuffing from spurs, as if the man had worn them occasionally, but not often. Not a riding man, he thought. The breeches showed some

18

sun fading, but there was no darker area where a gunbelt worn regularly would have protected the cloth. "He wear a gun much?"

" 'Course," Edwards answered. "He claimed he was Shea Glencannon, didn't he? With the name you've got yourself, folks'd expect him to wear one, wouldn't they? 'Specially the way your pa talked about you. Made you out to be a one-man hell on wheels. This feller had himself a new model Colt forty-five. Right fancy piece with carved bone butts. I got it in the office. Sporty handgun."

"It don't make sense," Glencannon muttered. He ran his fingers through the pockets of the dead man's vest. Nothing but tobacco, papers and a half-block of matches. The man hadn't been what he'd claimed, but there was nothing Glencannon could find to indicate just what he had been.

"You say my pa took him to be me?" That was the hardest part to understand.

"Yeah. He was introducing him all around town as you. We took his word for it, Shea. And the tales he was telling . . ."

Glencannon shook his head slowly. "Pa can't be more than sixty at most. Has he been sickly or getting weak-eyed or anything like that?"

"Jake? Nothing of the kind. He was prime man right up until — Shea, ain't you heard? You must have heard."

"Heard what?"

Edwards fumbled his hands together and looked down at them as if he had hold of something he wanted to get rid of, but he couldn't quite figure out how. Awkwardly, he said, "He's dead."

"My pa?"

He nodded toward the corpse on the cell floor. "That's what he was accused of. Murdering Jake."

Shocked, Glencannon stared at him.

Chapter 2

Edwards fidgeted uncomfortably.

Rising to his feet, Glencannon said slowly, "Fifteen years is a long time, Ted. After fifteen years the people you knew ain't quite real to you any more. I never heard from him. When I headed this way, I didn't know whether he'd be alive or dead. But . . ." He looked away from Edwards and nudged at the dead man's limp hand with the toe of his boot. "But *murdered.* And by somebody he took to be me. That's hard, Ted."

"Maybe it wasn't this feller who did it," Edwards offered. But he didn't sound like he really thought so.

"Just what happened?" Glencannon asked him.

Edwards sank down on the cell bunk. Leaning his elbows on his knees, he gazed at his knuckles. "Your pa kept rooms over the Oriental. This feller was staying there too. One night not a week ago, while the saloon was closed down for the night, folks heard shooting. They ran up to see what was happening and seen this feller ducking out of Jake's office. They found Jake dead at his desk. I got there and arrested this one. He wouldn't say nothing, not one way or another. Wouldn't hardly talk to me at all. But everybody was sure he'd done it. Jake had took two forty-five slugs in the chest. Killed him stone dead."

"Had this one been in town long?"

"Showed up three, four weeks ago. Closer to three I think. 'Bout the same time I'd heard rumors about you getting yourself killed down in Arizona. Took me by surprise, you — him — showing up that way. He moved right in with Jake and they went around together. That's when Jake done all the telling of fancy stories about you. And this feller kept showing off that gun of his."

"He use it any?"

Edwards shook his head. "He didn't have occasion to. You'd already got a fairly powerful name. Nobody around here wanted trouble with you. But after Jake was dead, I heard talk that him and this feller had quarreled a lot."

"What about?"

"This feller wanted Jake to cut him in on

22

a share of the place and he wouldn't do it."

"What place?"

"The Oriental. You've been over there. Didn't you know about that either?"

"I been away fifteen years," Glencannon answered. "I just got back. I ain't heard nothing."

"Your pa did real well for himself when the railroad was being built. When this town got to growing, he bought the Oriental and the hotel next door to it. Had money invested in other things, too, I hear. Did real well for himself."

Glencannon shoved the hat back from his forehead. He gazed at Edwards in surprise. "All that — that fancy saloon and the hotel and all — belongs to my pa?"

"Rightly only half belonged to him. He had a partner in it all. I reckon half of it'll be yours now. Or half of half, if I can find your brother."

"Dale? Is he still in these parts?"

"No. He took off with the railroad. Went off to Utah to operate a telegraph for 'em. I tried to send him a message when your pa was killed. Answer I got back, he'd quit his job and nobody knew where he'd took off to. I'm trying to find him, but I don't know if I can."

Glencannon studied on it. "Maybe that's

23

why this feller was claiming to be me. If he'd heard the talk that I was dead, and he knew he looked like me, maybe he figured he could cut himself in for my share by taking my name."

"But why would somebody up and murder him here in the jail?"

"Maybe he wasn't supposed to land in jail. Could be he wasn't alone in this. He might have had friends who didn't want him coming to trial and talking."

Edwards nodded in agreement, but he looked uncertain. "I ain't been marshal very long. This kinda thing's new to me. I don't know what to think."

"Maybe you ought to get a doctor or somebody and get him taken care of."

"Yeah."

"You mind if I look around? Maybe sign of some kind out back."

"I'd be obliged if you do, Shea. The way my head feels, I couldn't read shod tracks in fresh clay. I can't get my eyes to work to-gether," Edwards said. "I sure hope I ain't bad sick."

After he was gone, Glencannon searched over the body again. He could sense a wrongness. There was something he *should* see but didn't. He felt certain of it.

The backyard was fenced. The grass was

dry and sparse, with even drier earth under it. It would take prints only as dusty hollows. But there weren't any hollows. The ground under the cell window had been brushed over, like somebody had purposely wiped out any tracks.

There was a rain barrel at the corner. Somebody could have hauled it over and stood on it to look through the jail window. But the bone-dry bottom of the barrel was littered with sand and bits of dried brush. If anyone had upended the barrel that litter would have gotten dumped out, he thought with disappointment. He hooted into the barrel and listened to the echo, then turned into the alley between the jailhouse and the store next door. The dusty ground there had been brushed over too.

The way he figured it, someone had come back off the street, stood on something, poked a shotgun through the window and blasted the prisoner's head off. Then he'd retraced his steps, brushing them out as he went. That much seemed simple enough. But who it might have been — whether he was tall, short, fat or lean, booted or even barefoot — there was no telling.

He heard noises in the street and walked on through the alley. A crowd had begun to gather around the jailhouse door. Staying at the mouth of the alley, he leaned against the store wall and rolled himself a smoke.

Across the street, somebody'd put another horse next to his at the hitchrail. Like his mount, the animal was coated with road dust. He eyed the bedroll and warbag lashed behind the cantle and thought about his ride up from Arizona. He'd known he was being followed, but he'd never gotten a look at the hunter behind him.

He waited until Edwards came out of the jail, followed by two men carrying a blanketed bundle on a shutter. The crowd trailed after them up the street. Once they were gone, he crossed over to have a better look at the horse tied next to his.

It was a sorrel, as travel-grimed as his sandy bay, but not nearly so gaunted, as if it hadn't come as far or been ridden as hard. He didn't recognize the brand on its rump. But then whoever had been following him could have changed mounts along the way. And whoever it had been back there had gotten close enough to be here in Broken Crossing now.

He felt tempted to search into the saddlebags for some identification of the horse's rider. But there were too many people drifting back into the street. And it might be simple coincidence that had put this horse beside his own mount. Giving the bay an easy slap on the rump, he turned back toward the jailhouse.

The sense of wrongness still nagged at him as he looked the cell over again. But he found nothing to ease the feeling. Going into the office, he settled behind the desk to wait for Edwards.

After a few minutes of gazing at nothing in particular he started rummaging through the desk drawers. He found a heavy buscadero belt rolled around a holster sheathing a bone-handled Colt forty-five. The false Glencannon's gun, he thought as he stood up and unbuckled his own gunbelt.

The buscadero rig was stiff. Well-oiled but not used enough to be broken in. He tried it on, testing the set of the gun. Whoever'd positioned it had done it to his own taste. Not too low, angled just about right. He wondered if there could have been a mix-up of some sort: maybe the belt had been his pa's instead of the stranger's. No, Edwards wouldn't have made a mistake like that. It didn't make sense.

He put the gunbelt back, then poked into the next drawer. All he found was a sheaf of reward posters. He was thumbing idly through them, now and then pulling one out to throw it away, when Edwards came in.

"What you doing?" the marshal snapped.

"Your collection of reading matter here is a mite out-of-date. I've been sorting out the obsolete ones."

"You sure you ain't taking out the pictures of your friends from down to Arizona? Maybe looking for one of yourself?"

Edwards sounded like he meant it, Glencannon thought with surprise. He made a face. "You've been through these, ain't you, Ted? You ain't seen me here, have you?"

"I reckon not."

Curious, he asked, "If there was one, would you arrest me?"

"I took an oath when they gave me this badge," Edwards said slowly. He gazed at Glencannon, uncertainty in his face. "You find anything while I was out?"

"Nothing but dust and dry grass. And a few marks where somebody'd brushed out all the sign. Been a hard summer?"

"Driest in years. Wasn't there anything you could read?"

"Just that somebody had been and gone and didn't want anything about himself known. This weather puts me in mind of Arizona." Glencannon jerked the Bull sack out of his pocket and began to build a smoke. "You said my pa had a partner in all these businesses of his?"

The marshal nodded.

"Who is he?"

"Ain't a *he*. It's a *her*. Woman name of Liz Gerard."

Glencannon smiled slightly. "Good looking woman, huh?"

"Real handsome. I expect she's in her forties. Got a most-growed daughter. But you'd never guess it to look at her. Real handsome."

"Pa always had good taste. I think I ought to pay her a visit right soon."

"You'd better mind how you go calling on her. She's got a boyfriend running the business for her now. He ain't a feller I'd care to turn my back on."

"Oh?" He lit the smoke and looked up.

"Man name of George Carlisle," Edwards told him. "Blew into town a couple of months ago. Seemed to have known her before from somewheres else."

"How'd Pa take to him?"

"Not kindly at all. He ran Carlisle out of

the Oriental one night with the barkeep's Greener. Threatened to blow his head off if he ever showed up there again."

"And now *he's* running my pa's saloon for this woman?" The trace of a smile was gone from Glencannon's face. "Ted, what kind of checking around did you do after Pa was killed?"

"Not much," the lawman admitted. "It was all so plain and simple and there were witnesses and everything. At least — but how do you figure it, Shea?"

"I ain't sure. But maybe this fake was a friend of Carlisle's. Maybe he did the killing to get Pa out of the way, and then Carlisle killed him to keep him from talking too much at the trial. Could be the woman thought she could get hold of Pa's property and cut her boyfriend in."

Edwards considered. "It sounds sort of reasonable. But sounding good don't cut no mustard. I can't go accusing him without I got evidence."

"Then we'll get evidence."

"I dunno, Shea."

"Somebody had some reason for killing my pa. I intend to find out. Ted, you said the railroad didn't know what had become of my brother?"

"Uh-huh."

"If something's happened to Dale, too — look, for the time being, I'd sooner you didn't mention to anybody just who I am."

"What you mean?"

"I mean maybe somebody is going around killing off Glencannons. I'd sooner not get in line as a target until I've got some idea of what's going on," Glencannon answered. Rising, he flipped the cigarette butt into the spittoon. "I think I'll go calling on this Liz Gerard."

Edwards grabbed at his sleeve. "Listen, Shea, I don't want any trouble."

"Yeah," he grunted, turning toward the door.

As he stepped onto the walk, the brilliance of the midday sun struck his face. He paused, squinting against it.

Someone called his name.

The sound of it was high-pitched, harsh and hard as gravel. The meaning in it was knife-sharp. *Trouble.* The worst kind of trouble.

Chapter 3

As he wheeled, Glencannon's hand was already on the butt of the Colt. It cleared leather, the motion smooth, clean and quick as instinct. His thumb snapped back the hammer. His forefinger snugged against the trigger.

He saw the caller, blurred by the bright glare of the sun. A short, slim figure grayed by trail dust.

The two shots roared together, almost at the same instant. The gun jumped in Glencannon's hand. And the one the stranger held spat fire.

He felt the hat snatched off his head. He felt the hammer rising under his thumb. It fell again.

The stranger staggered back, as if slammed by an iron-hard fist.

Glencannon knew the third shot wasn't necessary, but his hand moved automatically. The gun bucked again. Lead bit into a wall plank, scattering splinters, as the stranger fell.

Behind him, he heard Edwards draw a sharp, startled breath.

Still moving as if of their own accord, Glencannon's hands ejected the spent shells, pocketed them, and reloaded the cylinder. And as he stood there, going through the automatic motions, he felt the cold tension like a snake that writhed in his belly. It was an ugly business. A hell of an ugly business.

Slipping the gun back into its holster, he stepped toward the prone figure. The people around him seemed to have been frozen in the instant of gunfire. His motion broke the trance. As he hunkered beside the body Edwards hurried to his side.

He put his hand on one outstretched arm. Under the dust-coated sleeve, he could feel the warm vitality of the flesh.

"Dead?" Edwards asked.

He shook his head. A sense of relief washed through him, lapping at the snake of tension in his gut. It began to slowly uncoil itself. As it eased, he realized what had happened to his hat.

There was a throbbing at his temple. He touched his forehead at the hairline. It was as if he'd laid a hot iron against his skin. Wincing, he jerked his hand away and looked at his fingertips. There was no blood.

It had been close, though. Awfully damned close. He frowned at the gun lying by the stranger's open hand. Softly he said, "He tried to kill me."

Edwards knelt at his side. In a thin, uncertain voice, the lawman asked him, "Why?"

He shook his head. There were a lot of possible reasons. He didn't know which one it might have been. Or even who this kid lying facedown on the walk was. But a slow, cold suspicion began to spread through him as he stared at the slender shoulders.

The kid's hat had been pulled down low. It was on snug. Glencannon jerked it off. Chestnut hair fell from under the crown in two long braids.

Edwards grunted incredulously.

With cautious, gentle hands, Glencannon turned the girl. Her face was gaunted and masked by sweat-caked dust. But he knew it well enough. Too well. With a silent curse, he asked himself why he hadn't realized who it was before he fired.

"A woman?" Edwards stared at the face, then looked toward Glencannon for some kind of explanation.

"She's still alive," Glencannon snapped at him. "Dammit, get a doctor!"

Edwards looked toward the crowd that had gathered. "Somebody fetch Doc Palmer. Hurry!"

A man broke from the mob and trotted off.

"Hurry!" Glencannon shouted after him.

The house was a white-painted cottage with a picket fence around it. The shingle on the gate-post read: RUFUS PALMER, PHYSICIAN AND SURGEON.

Glencannon carried the girl. She lay limp, unconscious in his arms. But he could feel the beating of her heart against his chest. It was steady and reassuring.

The doctor led them through a neat little sitting parlor into a room lined with shelves from floor to ceiling. It reeked of carbolic acid. At the doctor's orders, Glencannon put the girl gently down on the examining table.

Palmer nodded then, and with a wave of his hands sent Glencannon and Edwards back to the sitting room.

"Who is she?" the lawman asked, perching himself on the edge of a high-backed rocker.

Glencannon dropped onto a sagging

horsehide sofa. He leaned his head back and closed his eyes. In a voice that was almost a whisper, he said, "Sherry Grady."

"Why'd she want to shoot you?"

He didn't answer. Instead, as if he were talking to himself, he said, "She don't look much like I last seen her."

The rocker creaked as Edwards shifted around in it. He sighed and asked, "What's going on, Shea? What happened out there?"

"I shot her."

"Why?"

"She was trying to kill me."

"But *why?*"

Glencannon spoke with a slowness that sounded almost lazy. "I kinda killed her husband. Back in Gwinnett, Arizona."

From under narrowed lids, he saw Edwards start and stare at him. In his belly, he could feel the tension drawn into hard, painful knots.

"You wanna tell me about it?" Edwards said.

"No."

"I'm the law here! You just shot a woman out there on Grant Street. I gotta know what's going on."

Glencannon nodded as if he agreed. But he said nothing. The more he thought about it the less willing he felt to talk about it. He let his eyes close completely.

The rocker creaked as Edwards shifted impatiently, waiting for an explanation. Getting none, the lawman finally said, "Shea, we've been friends and I figure we still are. But if you're gonna make trouble for me, I can raise hell for you here in Broken Crossing."

"You reckon so?" Glencannon sounded only mildly interested.

"I'm not afraid of you and the name you've got for yourself!"

"You ain't?"

"No!"

"All right," Glencannon drawled. But he said nothing more.

The rocker squealed as Edwards twisted angrily. Then it was silent. Glencannon could hear the marshal's breathing. There was hard-won self-restraint in the way he sucked air into his lungs.

Glencannon thought as how he owed Edwards some kind of explanation. But not now. He couldn't talk about it now.

In the silence, his thoughts swung back to Sherry Grady. He hadn't recognized her standing there, masked by trail dust and the sun's glare. He'd only recognized the threat in her voice and the gun in her hand. And he'd fired at her — hit her. Now he waited for the doctor to come and tell him how badly he'd hurt her.

He asked himself what he would have done if he'd recognized her then. Would he have stood still and let himself be shot down? He didn't know.

Gwinnett had been a miserable town. A situation that bred misery. Men had died there. Good men like J. J. McKibbin. And a bastard like Charlie Grady. Glencannon had come close to dying there himself. It had been a war — an ugly, piddling little war for control of a stinking little town in a hell of a silver-rich desert — but still a war. Women had no place in war — not carrying guns and stalking men with the intent to kill. Not Sherry Grady.

Glencannon told himself that if Charlie Grady was so set on being the kind who'd get himself shot down, he'd had no right letting a woman love him that way. But the thought didn't change the facts. Charlie'd been a bastard, but Sherry had loved him. Now Charlie was dead, and Sherry hated the man who'd killed him.

Edwards spoke suddenly. "Shea, does the law want you back in Arizona?"

He thought about it. "Depends what you mean by law," he answered, with a bitter irony shaping the words. "The law in

Gwinnett is a dog-livered murdering son of a she-coyote name of Harry Wolfe who buffaloed his way into wearing a sheriff's star. He'd be real pleased to get his sights on me. But there ain't any warrants on me, if that's what you mean."

"That's what I mean."

Under his breath, Glencannon added, "None as I know of."

Edwards said nothing more. And the silence wrapped itself around them again. The creaking of the rocker just made it seem heavier. A clock ticking somewhere in the house added to it, like the sound of rats' teeth gnawing steadily into the afternoon.

Glencannon waited, feeling the knotted tension in his gut drawn and twisted. The silence was eating at him. He had to end it somehow. He put voice to his first thought. "You wouldn't know it from the way she looks now, but she's a real handsome woman."

"Who?" Edwards responded, startled from some far thought of his own. "That girl you shot?"

"Sherry Grady," Glencannon snapped as if the marshal had sinned by forgetting or not using her name. But then his tone softened again. "She used to work in the Loui-

39

siana House in Gwinnett. That's the fanciest place there. Real nice place. She'd sing and play on the guitar. Mostly the old kind of songs about true love and killing and things like that."

"In a saloon?"

He looked at Edwards angrily. "Not *that* way! She ain't that kind. It's just that she was such a handsome woman and had such a voice for singing. And Charlie — her husband — he worked in the saloon. He had her sing there to show her off. He was proud of her. But he'd of gunned down any man who tried to lay a hand on her."

"Is that how you came to kill him?"

"No!" For an instant, he was about to swing to his feet and throw a fist at the lawman. But he caught rein on himself. With a grunt, he settled deeper into the sofa and closed his eyes again.

He admitted to himself that in a mean, vicious way that shamed him, he'd been glad when Charlie Grady died. He'd been glad because he hated Charlie — hated the thought of Charlie having her — being loved by her. But that wasn't the reason he'd gone after Charlie. That was no part of it.

He allowed, though, that maybe it was

the reason he'd come here to Broken Crossing instead of going back to Gwinnett. Maybe he'd thought about Sherry and how she'd feel with her husband dead by *his* gun. Maybe that was why he'd run out.

He listened to the whine of the rocker and the slow death-march of the clock. The silence was thick and musty. He wished he could run now.

A doorlatch clicked. He opened his eyes as the door to the examining room swung open.

Dr. Palmer stepped through and stood, wiping his big bone-knuckled hands together. The eyes he held steady on Glencannon were dark amber and deep-probing.

Motionless, from under half-closed lids, Glencannon looked back at him, too taut to ask the question that tore at his thoughts.

As if he could read Glencannon's feelings, the doctor said, "She's going to be fine."

Those amber eyes disturbed Glencannon. He didn't fancy letting any man read too deep of his feelings. He tried to stifle the elation that flooded through him. Lazily, as if it hardly mattered, he asked, "How'd I hit her?"

41

"A clean shot through the serratus anterior, just under the deltoid."

"How's that?"

Palmer touched his hand to his side, just under the armpit.

"Didn't break no ribs?" Glencannon asked.

"No."

"She went down hard. Like she'd been buffaloed."

"She's a woman," the doctor said. "Not made of your fiber. And she was already weak, near exhaustion. Judging from those boy's clothes she's wearing, and the dust on them, she'd been traveling a long way on horseback. That can be plenty hard on a woman."

Glencannon nodded.

Edwards was leaning forward in the rocker. He rubbed his hands at his face, then asked, "Can I see her now?"

The doctor frowned at him. "Do you have a charge against her?"

He looked to Glencannon for an answer. "No."

"Is she likely to have a charge against him?" Palmer shot Glencannon a sharp glance.

"No," Glencannon muttered, hoping the guess was good.

Edwards offered, "He shot in self-defense. Everybody could see that."

The doctor seemed to consider it all. He said, "Then let her be for now. She needs rest. You can talk to her all you want later, when she's got her strength back."

Sighing, Edwards started to his feet. But he sank back into the rocker, pressing his hands to his head. "Doc, you got something I could take for a real rough headache and a kinda jumpy stomach."

"Hard night last night?" There was a hint of amusement in Palmer's voice.

"No! I had a couple of beers. That's all. You know I ain't much of a drinking man. Maybe I'm sick or something. Maybe I got the measles."

The doctor looked interested. He put a hand to Edwards' forehead, lifting an eyelid with his thumb. The eye was streaked with swollen red veins. "How'd you sleep last night?"

"Too good. Through the night and half this morning."

"Been feeling dull since you woke? Maybe a little chilly? Having trouble seeing straight?"

"How'd you know?"

"Had a sore throat?"

"No."

"Haven't been taking soothing syrup then?" Palmer stepped back.

Edwards knuckled his eyes as he grunted, "No. Never use it."

"Where'd you do your drinking last night?" The doctor sounded amused again. There was quickness, a cleverness, about him. Glencannon watched him with curiosity and a touch of admiration.

"The Oriental," Edwards said. He screwed up his face and blinked. "I didn't catch nothing there, did I?"

Palmer smiled outright. "Is Rudd Kelly riled at you for something?"

Blank and bewildered, Edwards shook his head. "Nothing I know of. Why?"

"It looks like somebody slipped you a shot of laudanum. You're about over it now, but I can give you a powder to ease the headache." Palmer disappeared into the examining room for a moment. He came back with a glass of fizzing liquid in his hand.

Edwards took it and gulped it down, scowling at the taste. Frowning, he mumbled, "Laudanum? Who? Why?"

Palmer took the empty glass from him and set it on a table. Turning to Glencannon, the doctor said almost smugly. "Now you."

"Huh?"

"While you're here, do you want me to take a look at those busted ribs?"

"Huh?" Glencannon grunted again. He gazed narrowly at the man. "What do you know about that?"

Chapter 4

Palmer was a clever man, and he obviously took pride in it. Grinning, he said, "I went through the war patching up holes in Billy Sherman's bummers and then I came West. I've followed hell-on-wheels railhead camps, worked cow towns and mining camps. I can tell easily enough from the way a man walks and draws breath when he's holding his ribs together with adhesive plaster. You want me to take a look at it for you?"

For a long moment Glencannon studied him. The doctor was big and raw-boned, reminding him of weathered red rock buttes. A clever man who could read deep into what he saw — but he knew nothing about what had happened in Arizona. Relieved at that realization, Glencannon got to his feet.

He peeled his vest and tugged out his shirttails. The swathe of adhesive plaster around his rib cage was wrinkled and dirty, coming loose at the edges.

"What would anybody want to slip me knockout drops for?" Edwards said suddenly. He sat frowning at the floor, looking at his own thoughts.

Interlocking his fingers, Glencannon rested his hands on top his head. He answered the marshal, "to put you to sleep."

"But why?"

"Maybe so you wouldn't hear that shotgun go off last night and run out to see who'd blown the head off your prize guest."

"That's strange," Palmer muttered as he forced the tip of a blunt-nosed scissor up under the tape and began to cut at it.

"Huh?" Glencannon looked down at the bandage on his chest, wondering what was wrong.

"I was here last night," the doctor said. "For a change nobody around Broken Crossing was snapping a leg bone, having a baby, or rupturing an appendix at the stroke of midnight. I spent a quiet evening reading and went to bed." He finished his cut and dug his fingers under the ends of the tape.

As he jerked, Glencannon winced. The adhesive came free, revealing a well-closed, slightly puckered scar.

"You mean you'd have heard a shotgun

fired off back of the jailhouse last night?"
Edwards asked.

The doctor nodded in reply to him.
Studying on the scar, he told Glencannon,
"Ribs are useful for deflecting bullets, but I
wouldn't try it too often if I were you."

"Wasn't my idea," Glencannon grunted.
"Maybe you were asleep when the shotgun
was fired? Maybe you sleep sound?"

"Not that sound. My bedroom's in the
back and my property butts up against the
jailhouse yard. If anybody fired off any kind
of gun there last night, I'd have heard it."

"That doesn't make sense." Edwards
sounded as if the strain of trying to understand was making his head hurt worse.

"No, it doesn't," Palmer agreed cheer-
fully. He prodded at Glencannon's ribs
and hummed deep in his throat.

"You always make noises like that?"
Glencannon asked.

The doctor looked at him blankly, then
grinned. "I didn't always. Learned it at
medical school. My patients expect it of
me. At least the fat civilized ones do. Who
dressed this bullet hole for you?"

Glencannon decided he liked the raw-
boned doctor. He grinned back and answered, "Feller in Navajo country."

"Indian?"

48

"No. White missionary on the reservation. A good man though."

"Use regular medicine or Indian medicine?"

"I dunno. I was out of my head for a few days. It bled a lot." That was probably how the rumor got started that he was dead, he thought. He'd spilled a mess of blood and ridden off into the desert. They'd probably figured he couldn't last long.

Palmer shrugged in disappointment. "I've heard a lot about the cures the Indians can work. Can't find out much about 'em though."

"Try living with 'em for a while," Glencannon suggested. "How's my ribs?"

"Sound and solid. You could've stripped that cinch a week ago."

"I was too busy to concern myself with it a week ago," he muttered. That was about when he'd realized he was being trailed. He scratched at his bared sides and asked, "Seeing as how I already got my shirt off, you mind if I wash up a bit?"

"Help yourself. There's running water in there." The doctor hooked a thumb toward a closed door. "Soap on the sink and towels in the cabinet next to it."

The sink had a faucet. Glencannon had seen the likes of them before in fancy hotels. He turned the handle, admiring the way water gushed out, without he had to heave a pump handle for it.

The water was tepid, but it felt good against his skin. He ducked his head under the faucet. When he was done, he stepped back into the sitting room.

Edwards was asking, "Doc, you sure you didn't hear a shotgun?"

"Positive."

"I just don't understand it."

The doctor shrugged.

"Knockout drops," Edwards mumbled, shaking his head.

"Evidently someone had some reason to put you to sleep and want you to stay that way," the doctor told him.

"Somebody at the Oriental," Glencannon put in. He picked up his shirt and pulled it on.

"Rudd Kelly?" Palmer suggested.

Glencannon asked, "Who's he?"

"The bartender."

"What would he want to give me knockout drops for?" Edwards said.

"Why would anybody do it?" Glencannon grunted. He turned toward Palmer. "That fancy water spigot, how's it work?"

"I've got a good well and a windmill.

Got a big tank on the roof. The windmill pumps water into the tank and when you open the faucet valve, gravity pulls it down again, through the pipes."

Glencannon thought about it, making a picture of it in his mind. "Who thought that up?"

"I don't know. It might have been the Babylonians. They had to have some way to water that hanging garden. . . ."

"Who?" Glencannon asked blankly.

"Babylonians," Palmer repeated.

"The ones in the Bible?"

He nodded.

"Damned clever," Glencannon muttered.

"There are a lot of clever people in this world."

"Yeah. And one of 'em was clever enough to blast the face off a man in the middle of town without anybody hearing the shot." He picked up his hat and set it square on his head. "Come on, Ted. We got us some things to look into."

Edwards got to his feet. He nodded to the doctor as he followed Glencannon toward the door. "Much obliged, Doc."

Palmer grinned at him. "Drop in again some time."

Pausing, Glencannon looked back.

"Doc, take good care of that girl."

"I will."

Outside, Glencannon led Edwards toward the corner of the doctor's house.

"Where we going?" the lawman asked.

"Just to take a look out back."

"What do you figure?"

"I don't figure anything just yet. I only want to look around." Halting at the side of the house, Glencannon looked up at the water tank. He muttered, "Clever."

"What?"

"That indoor plumbing. Come on." He headed back across the yard. Clambering over the fence, he studied the back side of the jailhouse. The doctor was right. It would be impossible for someone to fire a shotgun back there and not have it heard at Palmer's house.

Suddenly he dropped to one knee and picked up something from the sparse grass.

"What you got?" Edwards asked.

Glencannon held them up. "Chicken feathers."

"Huh?"

"Not just a couple. A handful. Somebody been stealing your chickens, Ted?"

"I don't keep chickens."

"Does the doc?"

"No."

"Well, it sure looks like somebody climbed over the fence here carrying a chicken. Striped dominicker."

"Somebody fetching back a runaway rooster," the marshal offered.

"Maybe." Glencannon shrugged and stuck the feathers into his vest pocket. "Maybe somebody muffled a shotgun blast with a feather pillow."

Edwards started. "You think so?"

"I don't know," Glencannon mumbled. It was an idea but it didn't quite suit him. A pillow might have muffled the blast, but it wouldn't drown it out completely. If there'd been a shot, even a muffled one, the doctor should have heard something, shouldn't he? He said, "Clever."

"The water tank?"

"That doctor. A real sharp-eyed feller. A doctor gets around a lot. Sees and hears a lot. That one especially. And I don't think he's the kind who'd spill out everything he's got in his head without a good reason."

"What do you mean?"

"I'm just wondering if he's got some reason for wanting us to think he didn't hear a shotgun. Look, Ted, you go send a telegram to the law where my brother was working last. See if you can get 'em to start

53

looking for him. I'll —"

"Don't tell me what to do!" Edwards snapped. "I'm wearing the badge. I'll do the lawman-work around here!"

"Huh?"

"You got no right telling me how to do my job!"

Glencannon gazed at him, deciding that it was likely nerves making him jumpy and irritable. Here Edwards was, fairly new to the job, and suddenly piled up with troubles that had him stymied. Likely he was mad at himself for being puzzled by it. "Sure, Ted," he said quietly. "I wasn't *telling.* I was *asking.* I'd be obliged if you'd get the law to looking for my brother."

"All right," Edwards muttered, still disgruntled. Drawing his revolver, Glencannon began to check the loads.

"What's that for?"

"Figured I'd head over to the Oriental and take a look at my new partner."

"Shea, if you figure on making trouble — the law's the law, friend or not."

"I got no plans for starting trouble. I just want to be ready if somebody else starts it."

"I don't want another shooting."

"Look, Ted, somebody murdered my pa and my name's been dragged into it. That gives me a hand in the game, don't it?"

Reluctantly, the marshal nodded. But he repeated, "The law's the law. You bust it, you'll pay same as anybody else."

"Sure," Glencannon agreed. He dropped the gun back into his holster and headed toward the street.

He wondered if this Liz Gerard and her boyfriend had been behind his pa's murder. It seemed likely. But how could a man as smart as Jake Glencannon let a double-dealing woman like that take him in?

Maybe it wasn't so hard to understand at that, he allowed as he paused on the walk in front of the jail. Once a man got his head full of notions about some woman, he could easy make a fool of himself. Or worse. He could hear a memory of Sherry Grady's voice calling his name. What would he have done if he'd recognized her? Stood there and let himself be shot down?

Jerking the brim of the hat down over his forehead, he strode on across the street. As he approached it, he studied the Grand Oriental Palace with fresh interest. He tried to picture himself presiding over such an establishment. It was hard to imagine. But then it was hard to think of his father running the place, too.

He recalled Jake as a rough, hard man dressed in greasy buckskins, cussing at him and his brother as he tried to teach them things. Jake had driven them both, forcing them to work at learning. He taught them to handle guns and horses, to stalk and survive in the wilderness. He'd never been easy with his sons, and he'd never won much in the line of love from them. But he'd had their respect and admiration. The murder had hit Shea harder than he would have expected. He looked at the saloon, wondering what his father had been like in those last years. Wondering what kind of woman could have softened the old man up and then killed him.

He shoved open one batwing and halted, letting his eyes adjust to the dimness inside the saloon. The place was still almost empty. Just a couple of men at a back table and a few more at the far end of the bar. He glanced at them, then looked around, taking in the layout of the room.

The bar ran along the wall at his right. To his left there was a door with pebbled glass panes. Likely it led into the lobby of the hotel. A staircase rose up the left wall to a wide landing. Far in the shadows, he could make out a back door.

He turned toward the bar, seeing the reflection of the room and the men in it in the backbar mirror. One of the men at the table was rising, heading toward him.

He recognized the stubby, swaggering figure of the fellow who'd sold him the watch that morning. Turning, he nodded in greeting.

"Howdy." Shorty spread a sort of amiable smile across his face. It came out looking more like a smirk. "I sure figured *you'd* have headed out of town by now. The law give you any trouble?"

"Why?" Glencannon asked blandly. "Should it have?"

"I heard there was a shooting scrape," Shorty drawled. In a voice like a tentative jab of a knife, he added, "With a *woman*."

Glencannon looked at the meaningless smile and the flat sly eyes. He wondered just what Shorty was trying to prod him into — and why? Without making a reply, he turned toward the bartender and called for two beers.

Shorty almost winced in surprise. But he picked up the drink the bartender set in front of him and took a long swallow. Then he grunted something at Glencannon that might have been a grudging thanks.

Nodding in acknowledgment, Glencannon glanced around and said sociably,

"Right fancy place. You're around here a lot?"

"Live upstairs," Shorty answered, puzzled.

"Like to keep close by, huh?"

"I work here. You might say I'm sort of an assistant manager." A bouncer, Glencannon thought. Hired tough. He said, "I forget now what you told me your name was."

"Steele."

It meant nothing to Glencannon. But he said, "That's a big name in these parts."

Shorty's grin became real with pride. "It sure is!"

"You work for Liz Gerard, huh?"

"I work for George Carlisle."

So the little man made a distinction between the saloon's owner and its manager. Glencannon had a feeling that was significant. But of what?

Shorty was watching him intently, waiting for him to pay for all that information with some of the same. Maybe an explanation. Maybe his own identity. But Glencannon offered nothing. He only drank slowly of his beer and gazed back at the little man.

Shorty's smile faded. He seemed to be recalling that he had business to tend to. He said, "Maybe now you'd be interested in buying one of them fast horses I got for sale."

"No."

"You're planning to leave right quick, ain't you?"

Glencannon shrugged.

"If you're smart, you'll get out quick."

"Why?"

"Climate around here might not be too healthy." Shorty's voice was cold. And there was something edging on fear in his eyes. He added, "Not for a man who goes around shooting down women."

Glencannon considered. The little man didn't give a hoot about his health, or the shooting. Shorty just wanted him to get the hell away from Broken Crossing. Why? What made Shorty fearful of Glencannon's presence here?

"I kinda like it here," Glencannon said.

Shorty's eyes narrowed down almost to slits. His mouth twisted as he started to speak.

A woman screamed.

Glencannon wheeled to face the stairway. She appeared suddenly at the top of the stairs, one hand clutching her skirts, the other pressed to her cheek.

Liz Gerard? Glencannon felt certain of it. He gazed at her as she paused for an instant. She was tall and slender, with bright yellow hair caught up in loose curls at the back of her head. Some of them had come free of the ribbon and were falling wild around her face. It was a handsome face with high cheekbones and a tapering chin. The brows arched sharply over deep, dark eyes. The eyes were tear-damp and the ruby mouth trembled and she lunged down the stairs.

She was the kind of woman Jake Glencannon would have appreciated, he thought, as he started toward her.

At the bottom step she turned to look up the way she'd come. Glencannon put a hand gently on her arm. Startled, she spun to face him. "Who are you?"

"Liz!" someone snapped.

There was a man on the stairs now. Liz Gerard turned back to stare at him: a tall, thick-set man who filled his suit coat with a broad span of shoulder. He wore his clothes well, with a confident ease. Pausing on the landing, he rested his hands on his hips. The gesture pushed back the skirts of the coat, showing a pair of Colts holstered butt-forward.

George Carlisle, Glencannon decided. Studying him over, he decided the Colts were more for show than use. Carlisle looked to be the type who'd produce a sleeve gun when he needed an arm quickly.

Standing in the domineering pose, Carlisle looked first at the woman, then at Glencannon. In a soft, lilting voice, he said, "Come on back upstairs, Liz."

"No!" She wrapped her hands around the banister as if she thought he'd try to drag her away by force.

The cheek she'd been covering with her hand was red. She'd been slapped. Hard.

"Come on, Liz," Carlisle repeated. This time his voice was not quite so soft.

Glencannon touched her arm again. To the man on the stairs, he said in a flat easy drawl, "If she don't want to go with you, she ain't going."

She winced and looked at him again, as if she'd forgotten he was there. Her eyes probed at him in silent question.

They were nice eyes, he thought. Hard-surfaced, but with a gentleness down deep. He had a feeling he could like her easily — if she hadn't murdered his pa.

Carlisle spoke. "This is none of your business, mister."

Glencannon stepped back, away from the woman. He let his hands fall to his sides. "*I* decide what is or ain't *my* business."

61

Carlisle's eyes darted, scanning the room, judging his situation. Maybe locating his close friends, like Shorty Steele.

With his back to the men in the room, Glencannon knew his own disadvantage. He shot a quick look at the backbar mirror. He didn't see Shorty's reflection. But there were others — plain, ordinary customers staring at the scene by the steps. They were the ones he'd depend on. Not for what they'd do if trouble broke, but for the witnesses they'd make. He didn't think Steele was the kind who'd shoot a man in the back — while there were witnesses.

From the expression that flashed across his face, Carlisle had come to the same conclusion. He stood motionless.

Glencannon waited, feeling the weight of the silence, aware of the inheld breaths of the watchers. He felt the tension curling in his gut.

"No!" the woman said suddenly. This time she spoke to Glencannon. Her hands released the banister. "No, don't. Not on my account. Not yet."

Lifting her skirts with both hands, she started up the stairs. She held her shoulders back and her head high.

Carlisle smiled slightly. He tucked a hand under her arm as if he were escorting her to a formal dinner. They climbed the stairs together.

Puzzled, Glencannon watched. What had she meant by *Not yet?*

Chapter 5

Glencannon turned. The regular customers were getting back to their drinks, their cards, and their talk. But two men were still gazing at him: the bartender and Shorty Steele.

Steele had moved over beside the door. But as Glencannon walked toward the bar, he headed back. There was still beer in the mug. Glencannon picked it up and took a sip. It was going flat.

"If I was you," Shorty said pointedly, "I'd mind my own business and move on. I wouldn't stay around Broken Crossing any longer than it took to pay up and get out."

Glencannon drained the mug and put it down. "Funny. If *I* was *you* I'd likely do just that."

The barkeep was looking at him like a man cornered by a snake who was wondering whether or not it had rattles on its tail. He fished out a couple of coins. Dropping them on the bar, he asked, "Where's there a decent place to bed a horse around here? For a few days, maybe a few weeks?"

He was watching Shorty's reflection in the mirror. The face barely changed. But there was a flickering of unhappiness in the little man's eyes. He looked like he was afraid a bad mistake was about to catch up with him.

"If I were you —" he started.

The bartender spoke loudly across his words. "Livery stable up to the north end of Grant Street."

"The folks in this town don't take kindly to a man who shoots women in the streets," Shorty persisted.

Glencannon didn't make any sign that he'd heard. But he knew Shorty was almost squirming. And the bartender was taking a lot of pleasure in the little man's discomfort.

"North end of Grant Street, eh? Up that way?"

The bartender nodded with satisfaction. Shorty wheeled, heading toward the staircase. Glencannon watched his reflection until he'd disappeared from range of the mirror.

Leaning toward the bartender, he asked softly, "Your name Rudd Kelly?"

Renewed suspicion narrowed the man's

eyes as he nodded in reply.

"I think maybe you and me have some business together," Glencannon said.

Kelly lifted an eyebrow in question.

"I think Marshal Edwards would be real interested in knowing why he got slipped knockout drops in here last night," Glencannon said, watching close for reaction.

Kelly looked like his snake had sounded its rattles. And showed its fangs for good measure. He took a step back, as if he could escape that way.

"What would it be worth to you to keep him from finding out?"

The snake had struck. Color drained from Kelly's face. He swallowed hard. His voice came hoarsely. "I don't know what you're talking about."

"You know damn well what I'm talking about," Glencannon answered with a grin he hoped was full of confidence. He wished to hell *he* knew what he was talking about.

Kelly was buying the bluff. There was terror in his eyes. But he tried again. "Mister, you're crazy."

"Sure. That's what Edwards'll think when I talk to him."

Looking down at his hands as if he expected to see blood on them, Kelly mumbled, "Not here. Not now. I can't talk to you now. Tomorrow. Maybe tomorrow." He lifted pleading eyes toward Glencannon. But the expression changed suddenly. He stared past Glencannon.

The reflection was in the bar mirror. Glencannon saw the two men who'd come down the staircase. One was Shorty Steele. The other a big, dark-faced, heavy-featured bull dressed like a jerkliner. They were both looking at Glencannon's back. Shorty gave a curt jerk of his head. The skinner nodded.

Glencannon let them get about halfway to him before he turned to face them.

The move startled Shorty. He paused. And decided to wait where he was while the muleskinner stepped up to Glencannon. Then he made a quick sidestep, moving toward Glencannon's right.

A flanking movement. The little man didn't play long odds. Glencannon watched the skinner, but kept an awareness of Shorty's position from the corner of his eye.

Raising a thick, dirty finger, the teamster pointed it into Glencannon's face. "I don't like you, mister." His voice was rough-edged, as if he'd worn it raw swearing at his mules. He spoke slowly. "I don't like no

67

man who goes around shooting wimmen."

Glencannon glanced toward Shorty. "What's got you so damn anxious to get me out of this town?"

Steele swallowed hard. He looked like something was caught sideways in his craw. He glared imploringly at the skinner.

"I don't like you," the big man repeated, balling his hand into a huge fist. Glencannon could read his thoughts — the planned swing — as easily as if it were all printed on his face like a circus poster.

The skinner swung.

Wheeling, Glencannon dove — not at the teamster but at Steele. His fingers wrapped around the little man's arm, biting in, hauling Steele off balance. With a twist of his body, Glencannon sent him careening across the floor to smash into the teamster. Thrashing, they went down together.

Glencannon stepped back against the bar, watching.

Shorty scrambled to his feet, one hand clawing for the butt of the gun at his hip. He'd been badly shaken by Glencannon's unexpected move. If he had speed with a gun, it didn't show now. His fingers trembled, hunting the gunbutt.

Glencannon waited. He knew his own

ability. He knew the tension drawing taut in his belly only served to hone the fine edge of his skill. He let Shorty locate the weapon with his fingertips before he moved.

It was smooth and snake quick. The Colt was suddenly in his hand, not aimed at anything exactly, but held casually, its muzzle pointing in Steele's direction.

Shorty's gunsight hadn't cleared leather. It didn't. His eyes locked to Glencannon's hand — and the gun in it. His shaking fingers opened, letting his own gun slip back down into the holster.

"I asked you a question," Glencannon said quietly. "You ain't answered me yet."

Shorty's face was blank.

"Why are you so anxious to get me out of town?" Glencannon repeated.

The little man's eyes darted, searching the reflections in the mirror at Glencannon's back. He saw the faces of the townsmen watching him. Color began as two small red spots on his cheeks. They spread until his whole face and neck glowed. He gazed at Glencannon with the particular hatred of a little man who's been made a fool of by a bigger man. Then he glanced past Glencannon at the mirror again.

Glencannon's back was against the bar.

He hadn't anticipated trouble from that direction. He read Shorty's fleeting glance though, and started to wheel.

But it was too late. Something slammed into his head. Pain exploded through his skull, a mass of sharp light inside his eyes. He felt himself falling and threw out his hands.

For an instant he was on his hands and knees. But something smashed into his right wrist, driving the arm out from under him. As he fell, it struck again, sending his gun skittering across the floor.

He was on his face, trying to raise himself on his arms. But a weight settled into the small of his back, forcing him down. He could feel the sharpness of a boot heel pressing into his spine.

He let himself lie motionless, eyes closed. The sparks of light inside his skull were fading and the shock of pain began to ease. He drew breath softly.

Shorty was laughing. It was high-pitched and tense, almost a giggle.

Glencannon bunched the muscles of his arms, bracing. Suddenly, he shoved against the floor, at the same time twisting his body.

The boot heel dug deeper for an instant, then slid across his back as Shorty was thrown off balance. The giggly laugh became a startled yelp.

Opening his eyes, Glencannon rolled. He saw Steele tottering on one leg. He grabbed for the ankle.

Shorty toppled like a felled timber.

Rising to his knees, Glencannon grabbed for the edge of a table. As he dragged himself to his feet, he shook his head, trying to clear it. His vision was blurred and the pain still sharp inside his skull.

He saw Shorty thrash, getting his arms and legs under him. He waited, letting the little man make it to his feet. Then he lunged, grabbing Shorty's shirtfront with one hand. Fisting the other, he swung.

There wasn't as much force in the blow as there should have been. Glencannon was aware of that, and of the soreness that had roused up in his scarred side. But his aim was good. His knuckles slammed into the doughy face, snapping the head back. Shorty's struggle against his grip on the shirt stopped.

He let go. The little man fell back, hanging against the bar for a moment. Then he slid down limply to lie like a puddle on the floor.

A shadow moved. From the corner of his eye, Glencannon glimpsed the motion. He turned as the teamster charged toward him like a bull-buffalo. It'd take a pole-ax to down that thick bulk. He knew he couldn't stand to the force of the skinner's drive.

Flinging himself under the teamster's lashing fist, he sprawled on the floor. His gun lay where Shorty had kicked it. His hand stretched toward it. Rolling, he caught it.

The skinner's momentum carried him several strides before he was able to stop and turn. As he wheeled, he saw Glencannon on the floor, propped on one arm, leveling the Colt toward him.

The click of the hammer coming at full cock was sharp and loud in the sudden hush.

Glencannon looked at the skinner standing like a befuddled bear, frowning in puzzlement. He looked toward the bartender with the snubbed-off Greener in his hands. He felt the heavy pain still in his head and knew what it was that had driven against his skull from behind. It was a big, ugly shotgun. The bores stared at him.

Above the gun, Kelly's face was white and taut. He was gazing at Glencannon with as much fear as threat.

Softly, Glencannon said, "That was a damned ornery thing to do."

"Put down that pistol," Kelly said thinly, gesturing with the Greener.

Ignoring the order — and the shotgun — Glencannon sat up. He kept the Colt leveled toward the muleskinner as he hefted himself to his feet. The snout of the Greener jerked and quivered, following his move uncertainly.

"You," he said to the teamster. He shrugged toward the door. "Go away."

The big man seemed incapable of moving. He stared, not even drawing breath, as Glencannon's words slowly penetrated. Then he broke, running. He slammed through the batwings. The hinges squealed as they swung wildly in his wake.

Glencannon turned toward the bartender. There was open astonishment in the man's face. Glencannon understood it well enough. A man like Kelly put his faith in being able to bluff down trouble with those twin barrels. When his bluff got called, he either pulled the trigger or else his nerve broke. Glencannon had put his own faith in Kelly's weakness. His guess had been good. He could see the tautness in the bartender's face — nerves frayed to the snapping point. Kelly was no killer. He'd back down and collapse under pressure.

Glencannon reached out with his left hand. Indolently, he wrapped it around the barrel of the Greener and twisted. As he tugged, Kelly's fingers opened, letting him take the gun.

He felt the snake of tension in his gut jerk like the snap of a whip. Anger surged through him. He hated it, the tension, the whole damned business of living by out-guessing sudden death. But there was no choosing another trail now.

He set the Greener down gently and opened his hand. There'd been blood on the barrel of the shotgun. It smeared his palm. There was more blood on the side of his head, where Kelly'd buffaloed him with the gun.

"That was a damned ornery thing to do," he said again.

Kelly stood like a statue, his empty hands still out in front of him. His face had all the vitality and color of a cold corpse.

Glencannon slipped the Colt back into his holster. Wordlessly, he turned and walked out of the saloon.

As he pushed through the batwings, the silent tension behind him broke. He heard the sudden murmuring of excited whispers. In no time at all, the story would have spread through the town. He was sorry for that.

Steele had said it earlier: Shea Glencannon had made a real mean name for himself raising hell in Arizona. As soon as the folks here realized he was Shea Glencannon, he'd have an ornery reputation for raising hell around here too. A mean name was a lot easier come by than a good one. Folks were always ready to think the worst of a man.

He wondered what the folks around here thought of Shorty Steele. And why the hell had Shorty been so eager to get him out of town? Did it have to do with his father's death? Did Steele know who he really was? He decided that wasn't likely. Steele would have spilled it if he'd known he was facing Shea Glencannon.

Shaking his head in puzzlement, he headed toward his horse. The dusty sorrel was still tied at the rail beside it. Thinking of Sherry Grady, he stepped between the horses.

He unhitched the sorrel, then his sandy bay. Forking the bay, he led the sorrel down the street, toward the livery stable.

Once the horses had been taken care of, Glencannon gathered up his gear and shouldered the girl's warbag. He headed for Doc Palmer's.

The woman who answered his knock seemed to be a housekeeper. She told him brusquely that the doctor was out and the girl patient asleep. Taking the warbag he offered, she slammed the door in his face.

Feeling weary, aching and dully discouraged, he turned toward the hotel.

Chapter 6

The hotel lobby smelled of furniture polish and stale cigar smoke. Glencannon halted inside the doorway, looking around. This place was quarter his now, too. But he wasn't ready to make his claim to it yet.

"Yes?" a small, tentative voice called to him.

The girl behind the desk was very pretty, but very young. Fine tow hair like a child's framed her face. It emphasized soft deep brown eyes that were all moist and innocent, like a doe's. Something about them struck him vaguely familiar. Wondering at that, he stepped toward her.

"Yes?" she repeated.

"I want a private room."

Her expression was as stern as a schoolteacher's. She glanced at the scruff of beard on his jaw, the dusty hat, faded shirt and tattered vest, with obvious disapproval. As if she thought it would change his mind for him, she told him,

"Dollar and a half a day."

It was a high price. But privacy always came high. He brought out a handful of coins. There were several eagles and doubles among the silver. The sight of them startled the girl. Glencannon knew why: he knew he didn't look like a man with gold in his pocket. Mildly amused by her surprise, he said, "I'll take it for a week."

She didn't answer, but studied him curiously. Her gaze traveled to the butt of the gun on his hip. And held there intently, as if she could read something from the gun.

When she looked at his face again, the surprise was gone. Instead there was something else — something he'd never seen in the eyes of a doe: a stark and intense hatred.

But it wasn't aimed at him. It was inward-turning as if it focused on something in her own thoughts. The sight of him had stirred some thought or memory in her that overwhelmed her.

What could make a young girl hate that way? he wondered as he chose an eagle from among the coins and flipped it onto the desk.

She hesitated, then picked up a steel pen and poised it over the register. "What's your name?"

"What's yours?" He figured he knew at least part of the answer already.

Her eyes narrowed. Slowly and distinctly, as if she wanted it to have meaning for him, she said, "Christy Glencannon."

It wasn't the answer he'd expected. Thoughtfully, he nudged at his hatbrim, shoving it back from his face. The world seemed to have suddenly become cram full of Glencannons. Trying to keep the puzzlement out of his voice, he said, "Glencannon? Like in Jake Glencannon?"

She nodded proudly. She'd been counting on his knowing Jake's name and being impressed by it. Why? He felt certain she didn't know he was Jake's son.

"You've heard of him!" she said eagerly, confirming her guess.

He nodded. "I knew him."

That struck sparks of excitement in her eyes. Almost breathlessly, she asked, "Were you friends?"

"Kinda," he mumbled, still bewildered by her. "But you're not more'n fifteen. Jake didn't have any daughter that age . . ."

"I'm almost sixteen!" she snapped, color rising to her cheeks.

"He didn't have any daughters that age either. Last I heard, he didn't have any daughters at all."

"That's just what you think." There was a hesitancy in her voice. She was lying and afraid he knew it.

He had a strong notion why her eyes seemed so familiar. He'd looked into eyes very much like them earlier that day. Grinning slightly, he said, "You sure your name ain't Gerard?"

The flush spread on her cheeks. But she held her defiant gaze on him. "Maybe Jake wasn't my real father. But he was the same as a father to me. I can use his name if I want. He wouldn't mind."

"Why do you want to?"

Thrusting out her small chin, she demanded, "What's it to you?"

He shrugged. Let her puzzle over it. Putting a finger on the eagle, he pushed it toward her. "You want to give me a key?"

She jerked one out of a pigeonhole and flung it down on the desk. "Illinois Room. Turn left at the head of the stairs. It's the third door to the back."

He picked up the key and started for the staircase.

"Hey!" she called after him. "You didn't tell me your name. I need it for the register."

He looked over his shoulder at her. "Glencannon."

She didn't believe him. He'd known she wouldn't. For a moment, he watched the anger and frustration blazing in her face. Then he headed on upstairs. She shouted at him again, but this time he didn't turn back.

He found the door marked *Illinois* and slipped the key into the lock. It turned sloppily. The door opened in.

It was a private room, all right. There wouldn't have been space enough for more than one person, unless he was uncommon friendly. A small table with a lamp on it sat next to the bed. There was a commode in one corner and a straight-backed chair in the other. The furniture managed to crowd the room and still leave it looking stark and bare.

Slinging the saddlebags over the foot of the bed, he pulled off his hat, then stretched out with his hands under his head. After a few minutes, he got up and poured some water into the basin on the commode.

There was blood caked in his hair where the barkeep had cracked him with that shotgun. When he washed at it, it bled a little more. But it didn't seem to be a deep or serious cut. Satisfied with that, he finished washing up, then pulled out the big timepiece and snapped open the lid.

The dining room ought to be open for business now, he decided. He stood listening to the watch play through its tune, luxuriating in owning such a fancy timepiece.

As he locked the door behind him, he was considering inviting Christy Gerard to join him for dinner. But when he got to the lobby, she was gone. A scrawny-necked man with a face like a turkey gobbler stood in her place behind the desk. Disappointed, he headed on to the dining room and ate alone.

When he'd done with dinner, he hunted up Ted Edwards. The marshal had nothing new to report. He hadn't gotten an answer to his telegram about Dale Glencannon yet. And he hadn't found anyone who'd heard a shotgun fired the night before. But he had questions about the fight in the saloon. He'd already heard the story in a dozen different versions. Some blamed the stranger. Some faulted Shorty Steele. Nobody seemed to know just why the fight had happened, though.

Glencannon gave the lawman a vague, only partially satisfactory explanation. Edwards was still complaining, wanting to know more, when Glencannon turned his back and walked out, grumbling, "I'll see you in the morning."

The sun was setting, and lights were glaring at the Oriental as Glencannon headed back toward the hotel. He considered stopping at the saloon again. But the weariness in his shoulders and the ache in his skull decided him against it. He didn't want any more trouble tonight. All he wanted now was rest.

The turkey gobbler was still behind the desk in the lobby. Glencannon gave him a brief nod. He didn't acknowledge it. *Real friendly, sociable town,* Glencannon thought as he climbed the stairs. But he had to own he hadn't gotten off to a very good start here.

He halted at the door to fish his key out of his pocket. But before he could thrust it into the lock, something grabbed his attention. Catching his breath, he listened. There was a faint sound of movement from within his room. Someone waiting in there . . . with a gun?

He took a cautious step back, then another, until he was even with the door of the next room. Bending, he looked through the keyhole. He could see the sky-glow of the window, but no lamplight. The room seemed to be empty.

Gently, he tried his own key. Like the

lock of the Illinois Room, this one was worn and sloppy. With a little twisting, his key worked it. He pushed the door open.

The room was about the same as his. There was no luggage, no sign of an occupant. Closing the door behind him, he went to the window. It opened with a thin screech of wood on wood.

Leaning out, he looked at the shutters. Then he climbed onto the sill. He clung to the frame as he reached out a foot to test his weight against the shutter holdback. It felt solid enough. Gripping the shutter, he swung out with his foot pivoting on the holdback. He flung himself toward the window of his own room.

Lunging through the open window, he dropped to the floor. He expected to draw the ambusher's startled fire. Rolling, he came up on his knees with his gun in his hand, the hammer back. The flash of gunfire would show him the whereabouts of the person hiding in the darkness. But there was no shot.

There was a scream.

It was a very thin weak scream that wouldn't have done a bit of good. It was too small to carry past the closed door.

"What the hell . . . ?" Glencannon muttered. His free hand went to his pocket for a block of matches. The other held the gun toward the source of the scream. He bit off a match and pocketed the block again. Awkward with his left hand, he struck the match.

It flared, filling the room with dull light and wavering shadows. The girl was huddled in the corner behind the bed with one small fist pressed against her mouth. She blinked against the light, then stared at the revolver leveled toward her.

"What the hell?" Glencannon repeated, rising to his feet. "Christy Gerard! What the devil are you doing here?"

She moved her hand away from her face and stiffened her shoulders. "I came to talk to you."

The reflections of the match were like tiny golden points of light caught in her eyes. She glanced at his face, then looked at the gun again. He realized he was still aiming it at her. Vaguely embarrassed, he dropped it into the holster and turned away from her to light the lamp. With his back to her, he said gruffly, "All right, talk."

When he faced her again, she'd seated herself on the side of the bed. She was gazing at her own hands now, and patting nervously at the folds of her skirt. Softly, as if she had trouble speaking the words, she asked, "You're a gunhand, aren't you?"

"Huh?" he grunted, startled. "What gave you that idea?"

"I can tell."

He remembered the way she'd looked at his scruffy clothes, his handful of coin, and the Colt he wore. She'd made an obvious guess, he thought. He asked, "What does it matter to you?"

"I want to hire you to kill a man."

What kind of crazy notion was that for a girl her age? Incredulous, he said, "Why?"

"Jake was the same as a father to me. I want you to kill the man who murdered him!"

"Somebody already did that," he said, thinking of the body in the jail cell.

She shook her head.

"You mean Shea Glencannon, don't you?"

"No! It wasn't Shea who killed Jake!"

Did she say that because she believed the man who'd been jailed hadn't been the killer, or because she knew the man wasn't really Shea Glencannon? He asked, "What makes you think he didn't do it?"

Twisting her fingers together, she gave another shake of her head. "I just *know* he didn't. Shea wouldn't have done anything like that. I knew him and I know he wouldn't!"

She meant she'd known the man who claimed to be Shea Glencannon, he thought.

"I don't believe all those other things they said about him either," she added. "He was good and kind and gentle and I don't believe he was any kind of killer. Not any time or anywhere! Not Shea!"

What had this name-stealer been anyway? What kind of man buckled on a gun and took another man's hellfire reputation to wear around town, and at the same time set a soft-eyed girl like this to pleading for him this way? Glencannon frowned in thoughtful puzzlement. And suddenly he was thinking of Sherry Grady spending all her love on a tramp like Charlie — even taking up a gun herself to draw blood for his death.

He looked at Christy. A half-grown girl with her head full of some kind of wild foolishness, coming to hide out in a stranger's room alone at night, trying to hire a murder done. Angrily, he considered telling her to get out of his room and forget the whole damned idea. But he held the words back. There was no guessing where she'd go or what kind of idea she'd get next if he just ran her out. And she might know things that he wanted bad to know himself. . . .

Jerking the chair away from the wall, he turned it and sat down astride it with his arm on the back. He rested his chin on his arm and gazed intently at her.

She looked back, solemn-eyed, and after a moment began twisting her fingers nervously together again. Finally she spoke. "Will you do it?"

"Do what?"

She looked resentful at his making her say it again. In a small voice, she worked the words out. "Kill George Carlisle for me."

George Carlisle. So the little girl figured it was Carlisle who'd murdered Jake. He asked, "You got any evidence that he did it?"

She shook her head.

"I don't think your mother'd be very happy if I just up and killed George Carlisle."

Surprise flashed in her face. "Why?"

"He's her — they're right good friends, ain't they?"

"Like hell!" the little girl spat.

"Huh?"

"Mama *hates* him. That's why Shea

came back. He was going to help Jake run Carlisle out of town. But they killed Jake and now they've killed Shea and — and —" Her words caught in her throat and tears formed on her lashes. Shaking free, they rolled down her cheeks. She pressed her hands to her face, trying to fight them back.

A sense of guilt surged in Glencannon, as if he were responsible for those tears. He had a notion to tell her who he was and what he was doing in Broken Crossing. But that would be a fool thing to do. Women, especially the young ones, had a way of saying exactly the wrong things at the wrong time and place.

"Look here, Christy," he said gently. "You've got a good honest marshal in this town. If it was George Carlisle who did those killings, Ted'll find out and get him brought to trial, all nice and legal."

She looked at him over the tips of her fingers. The deep brown eyes seemed to be accusing him of hurting her even worse with that suggestion. Snuffling, she said, "I'll *pay* you."

"Dammit, I'm *not* . . ." he jerked rein on his words, knowing she wouldn't believe him. She'd labeled him a killer and it fit the fantasy she'd built in her mind. She'd keep that label stuck to him until he offered her good reason to think different.

She was watching him, waiting. Some part of his answer must have shown in his face. Angrily, she snapped, "If you won't do it, I'll find somebody else who will!"

That was what he was afraid of. As she started to her feet, he said, "Hold on now! Is this something you've been planning about for a while? Or is it a notion you got into your head when I came in this afternoon?"

She glanced self-consciously down at her hands. The look was a guilty admission.

"Well, you think it over before you go talking to anybody else about it. You promise me that?" Rising, he worked the big watch out of his pocket and snapped open the lid. "It's past midnight already. You get yourself a good night's sleep and think it over tomorrow. Then you talk to me again before you say anything to anybody else. All right?"

She made no answer. She was suddenly staring at him with her face starkly pale under the tear streaks. Pressing her fist to her mouth, she mumbled something he didn't understand.

"Christy?" he started.

But she wheeled away from him. Jerking

open the door, she ran out like a panicked animal.

He almost ran after her. But he stopped himself. The girl was spooked badly. He'd frighten her even worse by taking off after her. If she were to start screaming she'd wake everybody in the place. And he'd have a helluva time explaining why he was chasing her through the halls at this hour.

He closed the door and tugged the time-piece out of his pocket again. Dangling it at the end of the chain, he studied on it. It must have been the sight of the watch, he thought. Nothing else — nothing he'd said or done — should have scared her that way.

Maybe she'd recognized the watch as having been Steele's. Steele worked for Carlisle. Had she assumed that because he had the watch now, he, too, was in cahoots with Carlisle? Maybe. But that answer didn't completely satisfy him. He wanted to talk to Christy Gerard again. But he had a feeling it wasn't going to be easy to get the opportunity.

Chapter 7

The sky beyond the window was a brilliant blue. Somewhere outside a rooster shouted his sun-welcome. Glencannon opened his eyes, stretched and yawned. As far as he was concerned, the new day was as welcome as a poke full of polecats.

He lay still, taking account of himself. There was a dull throbbing in the side of his head, his shoulders ached, and his belly felt like a dry well. At least the empty belly would be easy enough to cure, he told himself as he sat up. Leaning his elbows on his knees, he yawned again and rested his face in his hands.

He'd dreamed of Christy Gerard calling him killer. Now the feelings of the dream echoed unpleasantly in his mind. He told himself he shouldn't let it bother him. After all, he'd chosen his own trail and put effort into making a reputation. He'd worked hard to look like a man who shouldn't be tangled with.

That had been important back when he worked for the Overland. And even more important when he'd quit that to throw in his lot with J. J. McKibbin. J.J. had a pretty fierce reputation, too. But J.J. was dead now, and Glencannon didn't want to think about him, or about the job they'd gone to Gwinnett together to do — the job he'd left unfinished.

He dumped water into the basin and splashed some into his face. Studying his image in the mirror, he wondered about shaving. His father had usually sported full moustaches, but generally kept a clean-scraped chin. He was usually clean-shaven himself. But without the scruff of beard on his jaw now, he'd probably show a lot more family resemblance to his pa. No advantage in that. He scratched at the whiskers and turned to dig his clean shirt out of the saddlebags.

As he dressed, he considered the day ahead. After breakfast, he was to meet Ted Edwards. They were planting the remains of the man who'd claimed to be Shea Glencannon and had gotten himself killed doing it. Ted said the doctor usually helped with affairs like this, but Palmer had been called off on some kind of emergency, and Ted would need help handling the box. So Glencannon had agreed to give a hand. He felt mildly curious about the funeral. And in a vague way he felt almost an obligation to go. After all, it was *his* funeral.

Delays piled up one on top of another. Palmer had left things in good order, with the lid nailed on the box already. But when they arrived at the graveyard, the old man hadn't finished digging the hole. Then the preacher was late. The sun rose higher and hotter while they waited. The air thickened with dust and mosquitoes came in droves.

Once the sky-pilot got started, he built up a fair head of steam. Considering that he was saying almost nothing at all about a man he'd never known, he managed to drone on and on. By the time he got to the last *amen*, his small audience was shuffling restlessly.

Glencannon had begun to be sorry he'd come at all. On top of everything else, the preacher kept referring to the dead man as Shea Glencannon. After the first couple of times, he found that it bothered him to hear his name used that way.

As soon as the affair was over, he grabbed Edwards' arm. "We got our horses. The grave digger can take the wagon back without us, can't he?"

"I guess so," the marshal mumbled.

Glencannon started toward the clump of trees where they'd left their mounts tied — and stopped in midstride.

A third horse was there in the shadows. A sorrel with a slim figure in the saddle. She wore boy's clothes and she sat astride, but there was no hat covering her hair now, disguising her.

She shouldn't be here, Glencannon thought, gazing at the sling that held her right arm. *She shouldn't be up and around when she was still weak with that injury.*

"Glencannon!" She called it out sharply, with bitterness and hatred in her voice. But this time it was no gun-challenge.

He strode toward her. Fighting the emotion that might show in his face, he looked at her questioningly.

"How did you like it?" She snapped out the words like the crack of a whip. "How did you like watching your own funeral that way? A shoddy pine box and nobody to mourn you. Not one single tear."

"*My* funeral?" he muttered, knowing what she meant.

"Yes! Here in your own town. People thought it was you in that box. They'll put *your* name on the grave. *Here lies Shea*

95

Glencannon, dead and buried and nobody gives a damn." She paused, glancing toward the old man who shoveled dirt into the grave as carelessly as if he were filling a privy hole. Then she looked at Glencannon again. "But that's wrong. I'd give a damn. I'd sing and dance and tell this whole stinking world how much better off it was without you!"

"Ma'am!" Edwards stared at her, shocked by the intensity of her hatred.

Her voice softened as she looked past Glencannon, into her own memories. "Charlie's funeral was beautiful. Fellers came in from all over the county. There were silver handles on the coffin, and a white satin pillow for his head. Harry had it sent in from Tucson. Harry did real well for Charlie."

After Charlie was dead, Glencannon thought bitterly. Didn't she understand Harry Wolfe at all? Didn't she know the showy funeral wasn't for Charlie, but a big act for the rest of the men that Harry Wolfe might someday be sending to their graves?

He untied the sandy bay's reins and stepped up to the saddle. Swinging the horse around so that he faced the girl, he said, "You'd better ride back with us. You got no business being out here alone."

"Ride with *you!*" She made it sound as if he'd suggested something vile and indecent. Turning to Edwards, she spoke to him, but her words were still for Glencannon. "He murdered my husband back in Arizona. He hunted him down like an animal and slaughtered him! You think I don't know why?"

The marshal gazed at her blankly.

"You think I never saw the way he looked at me?" she went on, her voice growing shriller. "You think I never saw the murder in his face when he looked at Charlie?"

Glencannon's hand tightened on the rein until his knuckles were white. He'd taken as much as he could of her tongue-lashing. More than he could take. He had to stop her — somehow. With a touch of the spurs, he shoved the sandy bay up against her sorrel.

"You think I —" The words died in her throat.

Leaning out of the saddle, he caught her mouth with his — suddenly and fiercely.

She struggled against him, scraping at his cheek with nails too short to cut deeply. She fought and he grabbed at her hand, locking his fingers around her slim wrist.

For a moment, he was caught in a fantasy — in the dream he'd built from nothing. He tasted the warmth of her mouth. Even the small sharp pain as her teeth found his lip and dug into it was sweet. But there was no yielding in her. She returned nothing — but fought desperately against him. The dream died.

He eased his grip on her wrist. She pulled, sliding her hand through his, jerking her head back.

"Shea!" Edwards was gasping in horrified astonishment.

As Glencannon freed her, the girl wheeled her horse and drove her spurs into its flanks. It leaped, half-bucking, stretching its legs into a long gallop.

Over her shoulder, she spat a single word at him. *"Murderer!"*

Edwards had grabbed for his own horse. Catching a stirrup, he swung up and raced after her.

The sandy bay danced its forehooves, eager to join the chase. It tossed its head against the bit that Glencannon held firm.

He sat the prancing horse, watching the two of them galloping toward Broken Crossing. What the hell had he expected of her? he asked himself. He knew well enough how she felt about him.

Reluctant to ride on back to town, he turned and ambled the horse toward the gravedigger.

The box in the hole was completely covered now. The man in *his* grave was buried.

Pausing to lean on his shovel, the gravedigger let fly a wad of tobacco juice and eyed Glencannon with amusement.

"You do this kind of work regular?" Glencannon asked him. "I mean digging graves."

The old man bunched his cud in one cheek and said, "As regular as there's call for it."

"Been doing it for long around here?"

He frowned as if he were counting inside his head and it was a job of work. "Eight, ten years, I reckon. It ain't much for a feller my age."

Glencannon cast about for another question, something to say just for the sake of talking. "What'd you do before?"

"Nigh everything there is for a man to do. And mebbe more." The old man smiled as if it gave him a lot of pleasure to recall all the things he'd done in a long lifetime.

"Ever kill a man?"

"More'n one." He spat again, wiped his

mouth with the back of a gnarled hand, and grinned. Only one tooth showed, and it was a tobacco-stained stump. "Kilt Injuns and kilt Rebs. Mebbe some others besides. Never shot a woman, though."

Glencannon winced. He searched the old man's face, but saw only amusement in it.

"Always admired wimmen myself," the gravedigger mused. "Had six of 'em. Two white wimmen, a Chinee gal, two Blackfeets and a Sioux."

"All at once?"

"Nope. Never more'n one or two at a time. They're all gone now. Dead, I reckon. 'Course, they was only my regular wimmen. There's been plenty more I had a passing fancy for. I reckon I've bedded more prime beef than you've ever seen, young feller."

"That's a lot of wimmen."

"I been around a lot longer'n you have. Came here eight, ten years back. Before that I covered every mile of land betwixt the Platte and the Rio by foot. And I been around the whole world twice, sailing merchant ships."

"You've covered a mess of country."

The old man nodded. "Nigh all there is. And I've bedded every kind of woman there is."

"Was there ever one got into your head and you couldn't stop thinking about her?"

"Six," he grinned. "Two white wimmen, a Chinee gal, two Blackfeets and a Sioux. The rest was just passing fancies." He picked up the shovel and dropped another clod into the grave.

Glencannon sat watching silently. After a moment, the old man leaned on his shovel again and asked, "That she-male in the britches?"

"Huh?"

"That she-critter on the sorrel horse — is she the one that's in your head?"

When Glencannon didn't answer, he continued, "You think I didn't see the carryings-on down yonder? I may be old but I ain't blind. The way she rid off with that friend of you'n, I reckon she thinks mighty high of you, too." He gave a thin cracked cackle.

"Oh, she does. She surely does," Glencannon grunted. "She thinks I'd make a real fine corpse."

The old man shifted his cud and said proudly, "I never yet seen a young scamp like you as knew a thing about how a woman thinks. The worse they treat you, son, the more they like you."

"She'd like to sieve my gizzard with lead."

"Tried to shoot you once already, didn't she?"

"Yeah."

"It happened to me a time or two. True love, that's what it is. I know."

Glencannon snorted.

"Well, you take my word or leave it. Ain't nothing to me what you do," the grave-digger told him. "But when I was your age, I was a bull-grizzly with the hair on the inside and if there's anything I know, it's wimmen."

"You don't know that one," he mumbled, lifting rein. As he turned the bay toward town, he could hear the old man's cackling laughter. *Crazy old coot,* he thought as he put spurs to the bay's flanks.

The image of Sherry Grady clung to his mind. Even at a gallop, he couldn't escape the memory of her mouth, the feel of her hand under his.

Jerking rein suddenly, he stared at his own right hand. The bony knuckles were scarred, the lean tanned fingers callused. A knowledgeable person could read things about him from that hand. The lay of the calluses said that the hand was accustomed to using a revolver.

There'd been calluses on Sherry Grady's hand — a small slick layer of thickened skin on the tip of each finger. The man they'd just buried had the same kind of calluses, but his were on the *right* hand. Sherry's were on the left.

Lifting rein, he hurried on to town. He stopped first at Dr. Palmer's, but the housekeeper told him the doctor wasn't back yet, and neither was the girl.

He found Sherry's sorrel tied at the rail in front of the jailhouse, next to the dark bay geld that Edwards had been riding. A rap at the marshal's door brought no answer. He tried the knob. The door swung in onto an empty office.

Puzzled, he started along the plank walk, glancing into windows and wondering where she could have gotten to.

He'd gone the length of the walk down one side of Grant Street and was almost halfway up the other side when he spotted them.

The place was a flyblown little café where teamsters would drop by for pie and coffee. It wasn't the sort of place to take a lady. But then a woman in britches wouldn't get the treatment there she'd be in for if she tried to go into some respectable eating place.

They were sitting at a back table, well away from the window, but the light blur of

Edwards' pale blond hair caught Glencannon's eye. The marshal's back was to him. But the girl saw him step through the doorway. She leaned across the table to whisper something to Edwards.

He jerked around, rising out of his chair as Glencannon came up to them.

"Shea," he started, scowling darkly, "if you mean to . . ."

"Hold on. I come to talk to you and the lady."

"There's nothing *you* have to say to her." Color was beginning to rise in Edwards' face.

Glencannon ignored him. Hooking his thumbs in his pockets, he looked in question at the girl.

The hatred was still hot in her eyes but her lips turned slightly, hinting at a smile. A very smug, self-satisfied smile. "If you've got something to say, go ahead, say it."

That little smile was all wrong, he thought. She had some kind of hole card she was planning to spring on him. But what?

"You've got calluses on your hand," he said. "On the tips of your fingers. That's from playing the guitar, ain't it?"

Bewildered by the question, she nodded.

"They're only on the tips of your *left* fingers, ain't they? The fingers you hold the strings down with?"

She nodded again.

"What the devil are you getting at?" Edwards snapped.

"Would a feller play the guitar backwards? I mean getting those calluses on his right hand," Glencannon asked the girl. "Would he do that and still do other things the regular right-handed way?"

"What other things?" the marshal asked.

This time Glencannon answered him. "Like drawing a gun."

"I don't think so," Sherry said slowly.

"Why?" Edwards demanded. "What are you talking about?"

"That feller we planted this morning. There's something all wrong about him. I ain't got it all figured yet. But maybe if you and me were to sit down peaceable and talk about it . . ." Glencannon glanced past the marshal at the counterman who leaned forward, listening avidly. "Let's us go over to your office where we can talk in private."

Sherry Grady reached out to touch Edwards' hand lightly. She gave a slight shake of her head.

"Later, Shea," the marshal mumbled, gazing at the girl.

Glencannon started to argue. But he knew it was no use. There was no point in trying to reason with a man when he was involved in looking at a woman the way Ted was at Sherry.

And the look she'd given Edwards — that sweet, warm, honey-stay-here-with-me look. Was that real, or part of the game she was playing?

Either way, it rankled him. Disgusted, he wheeled to stride out of the café.

Chapter 8

Hooking his thumbs in his pockets, studying hard on his own thoughts, Glencannon strode down the plank walk.

Everything was sour to begin with, and getting worse. The troubles in Broken Crossing were mixed up enough without Sherry Grady complicating them by making eyes at the marshal. What did she figure that'd get her? Did she have some notion she could convince Edwards that her husband's death had been murder?

Dammit, why couldn't she understand?

Her face with that small smile, as if she looked at him over a gunsight, was in his mind. He didn't see Christy Gerard barreling out of a doorway, her own attention on someone inside the store. She rammed into him and stumbled.

Automatically, he reached to catch her. His hands locked on her shoulders, steadying her. She turned toward him then — and screamed.

It was a piercing knife of a yelp that startled him worse than being walked into. Releasing his hold on her, he stepped back.

She screamed again. This time her cry made a word.

"Murderer!"

He'd been whipped with that name already. When she lashed it at him, it cut raw and deep. He grabbed for her again, his fingers digging deep into her upper arm.

"Christy . . ." he began. But she screamed again. And kept on screaming. There was stark terror in her face.

Scowling in puzzlement, he tried again. "Christy . . ."

Something dropped heavily on his shoulder. A voice like the grate of a dry axle roared at him. "Let her go!"

Turning, he glimpsed the man — and the fist. The man was a broad, bulky redhead. The fist was coming at his face.

Instinctively, he jerked away from it. The knuckles brushed his jaw, glancing. And his own clenched fist lashed out. It hit hard belly muscle.

Grunting in pained surprise, the redhead backstepped. Lowering his head, pressing his chin against his chest, he lunged toward Glencannon like an oncoming freight train.

Glencannon pivoted, letting the big man's momentum carry him past. He came up against the hitchrail almost hard enough to topple it. The tied horses snorted and jerked at their reins. One broke loose.

The redhead clung to the rail, catching breath. Then he turned. His face was nearly as red as his hair. Balancing on the balls of his feet, he growled like an enraged animal, and lunged again.

Sidestepping, Glencannon swung a fist. The redhead's guard was high. Glencannon caught him in the gut again.

The shock of the blow jolted Glencannon's whole arm. It halted the redhead and held him, shuddering, for an instant.

Glencannon swung the other fist up. It slammed at the man's jaw, jerking his head back. He staggered, backstepping, shaking his head groggily.

One more, Glencannon thought, starting to follow him. But suddenly there was a hard pressure against his back, square between the shoulders. And a sharp click that he recognized for the cock of a gun hammer.

He froze.

The redhead stood, legs apart, gasping deep breaths and frowning as if he were bewildered by the course of the fight.

"What the devil's going on here?"

Glencannon recognized Ted Edwards' voice. Cautious of the gun prodding at his back, he turned his head enough to see the marshal shoving through the crowd that had collected.

Sherry Grady was close behind Edwards. She looked at Glencannon with a grim pleasure.

"Tate," the marshal snapped, "put that iron away before somebody gets hurt."

Glencannon felt the gun muzzle withdrawn from his spine. He turned then, looking for Christy Gerard.

A heavy-built, well-dressed woman was holding the girl to her bosom, patting her back as she sobbed.

"Christy," Glencannon said.

The girl lifted her head. Staring at him through her tears, she gasped, "*You!* You killed Jake!"

"Huh?" Edwards grunted. He looked from Christy to Glencannon.

"Marshal, *he* killed Jake!" She thrust out an arm, aiming a finger at Glencannon. "*He* did it!"

An ominous mumbling rumbled through the crowd. It was a sound that sent prickles of ice down Glencannon's spine. He'd seen mobs before.

Calmly and quietly, he said, "Christy, I wasn't even near Broken Crossing when Jake was killed."

"You did it! I can prove it," she insisted.

"You take it easy," Edwards stepped toward her. "You're all excited and you're wrong. He ain't the one who killed Jake."

"But I can *prove* it!"

"Ted, when was Jake killed? About a week ago, didn't you say?" Glencannon asked.

The marshal nodded.

"Well, I got at least one witness who can tell you just where I was a week ago. And likely every day after that right up till I got to town yesterday. You know that." Glencannon glanced significantly toward Sherry Grady.

She knew what he meant all right. He could see the sudden angry frustration in her face. She'd been close enough on his trail to know he couldn't have done any killing here a week ago. And as much as she might like the idea of seeing him hanged, she couldn't tie the knot herself with a lie.

"Yeah," Edwards muttered. It seemed to rankle him that Glencannon had pulled Sherry into this. He swung around to face the crowd. "You folks get! All of you get on back to your business. I'll take care of this."

Glencannon rubbed at his knuckles and watched as they spread slowly to drift back wherever they'd come from.

"Christy," the marshal said, "you come on with us over to my office. I'd like to know just what kind of proof you think you've got against Sh— against my friend here."

The girl looked solemnly at Edwards. "Is he your *friend?*"

"Yeah."

She shook her head uncertainly. "But he's got Jake's watch. He must have killed Jake and stole it off him. Carlisle paid him to kill Jake. I *know* he did."

"*Jake's* watch?" Glencannon touched the pocket with the timepiece in it. "Christy, are you sure of that?"

She jerked back, frightened of him. This time it was Sherry Grady who reached out a comforting hand to her.

"Leave her alone, Shea," Sherry snapped. "Can't you see you've got her scared sick?"

He gestured helplessly.

"This poor child's too upset for you to be prodding at her," Sherry went on. "Ted, we'd better take her home. You understand, don't you?"

Edwards shrugged and glanced toward Glencannon. "She's right. We'd better take Christy home now. Let her calm down 'fore we go asking her a lot of questions. You wait for me in my office."

"All right," Glencannon mumbled. He didn't like the way Sherry seemed to have the marshal on the bit. It looked like she had a good enough grip to pull him any which way she wanted. And the direction she wanted was obviously away from Shea Glencannon.

In the office, he settled himself behind the desk to wait. And time dragged slowly past. He began to wonder if Sherry'd hauled the marshal off in some other direction now, instead of letting him come back to the business at hand.

The knock at the door was small and timid. It sure wasn't Edwards.

"Come on in," Glencannon called without stirring.

The door opened a crack, held, then swung farther and Christy Gerard crept in like a rabbit nosing around a bait. She stood poised, ready to bolt, and said cautiously, "They called you *Shea*."

He nodded slightly.

"Can I talk to you?"

"You mean to get me into more trouble?"

Shyly, she shook her head. "I'm sorry."

He grinned at her.

She smiled slowly and uncertainly. But some of the tension in her drained away. "I'm awful sorry. The marshal told me you got that watch from Mr. Steele. He said you showed it to him when you first got to town. And the lady said you were down south of here when Jake was shot."

"So you're sure now it wasn't me that killed him?"

"Yes, sir." Her eyes were big and solemn and intent on him. "If *you're* Shea Glencannon, who was *he?*"

"First you figure I'm some gunhand you can hire to do a killing. Then you decide I killed Jake. Now you got a notion I'm Shea Glencannon," he said.

"They called you Shea. I kept on thinking about it after they left me at home. I kept remembering *him* and how he wasn't at all like people said Shea was. And — and you kinda — you look like you'd be Shea Glencannon."

He snorted, not sure whether to be amused or insulted.

"But if you're Shea, who was he?" she said again.

"I'd like to know that myself," he mut-

114

tered. "You were pretty good friends with him?"

"Uh-huh."

"Did he ever say anything to you about where he came from, or name anybody he knew outside of town, or anything like that?"

"No," she answered thoughtfully.

"Did he ever play a guitar while he was around here?"

"Not that I know of. Why?"

"Did you notice was he right or left-handed?"

She studied over it. "Right-handed."

"You're sure?"

She nodded.

He worked the Bull sack out of his pocket and built himself a smoke. Then he asked, "You recall anybody around here who played guitar left-handed? Backward, with his right hand up on the strings and his left hand doing the plucking?"

"Sure. He wasn't anybody in particular though. Just some drifter. Lots of drifters come through town. Some of 'em stop at the hotel."

"Did he?"

She nodded again. "He took a bed for the night, only he never slept in it. It wasn't touched when I went to make it up the next morning. I never saw him but that one day. Why?"

"You recollect what he looked like? Was he dark-headed, maybe about my height, but heavier built?"

"I guess so. Only he was older'n you. A lot older."

Glencannon figured that didn't rule him out. He asked, "Tell me about him, Christy. Everything you remember."

She sighed as she thought about it. "He came on the stage from Laramie four or five days ago. I saw he had a guitar with him when he came into the hotel. After he paid for his bed, he went into the saloon and I sneaked over and opened the door a little ways." She paused, embarrassed. "I just wanted to hear what he played. I like music. I listened at the door, and I seen him play the guitar backward like you said. I'd never seen anybody do that before. It was like looking at him in a mirror."

"And after that?"

"After he'd sung a couple of songs the men begun buying him drinks and such, and I figured I'd best get away from the door before Mama caught me at it. I didn't see him again after that at all. When I went to make up his bed, he hadn't slept in it."

"What about his belongings? He didn't

116

maybe leave them in the hotel?"

"No. They were all gone. Like he up and left town as sudden as he came."

"Maybe he didn't ever leave," he muttered.

"What?"

"I got some ideas, Christy, but I ain't got 'em sorted out to make sense yet. You tell me what you know about George Carlisle."

"Not much. Mama don't want me to have anything to do with him. And I don't want to either. Mama hates him. So did Jake." She looked at him curiously. "You will kill him, won't you?"

He swung his feet down off the desk and leaned toward her. "Christy, I don't know just what people have been saying about me around here, but I don't go around killing off men like so many head of diseased beefs."

"But you're *Shea Glencannon!*" She said it as if it made him ten feet taller than anybody else and entitled him to do whatever he pleased.

"Being Shea Glencannon don't set me above the law," he said.

"Are you afraid of the law?" It sounded more like an accusation than a question.

He fished into a vest pocket and tossed something down on the desk in front of her. It was a deputy marshal's star.

"You see that?" he said firmly. "The man who gave me that to wear was my best friend. And the best lawman you'll ever hear of. His name was J. J. McKibbin and he got himself shot down trying to make tin stars like that mean something. You've already got decent honest law here in Broken Crossing. If you want to keep it that way, you've got to respect it. You leave the law do the worrying about George Carlisle."

"But, Shea —"

"Christy, if Carlisle was responsible for killing my pa, then Ted Edwards and me will get him. But we'll do it as legal as we can." He picked up the badge and slipped it back into his pocket, muttering, "I got a kinda obligation to that star."

There was admiration and awe in her gaze as she nodded. Whether she'd understood or not, she accepted his decision.

And suddenly he felt guiltily self-conscious, remembering the job he'd left unfinished in Arizona.

Chapter 9

Glencannon had long since sent Christy home. He waited impatiently in the office as the afternoon stretched into evening. But still Edwards didn't come back.

He figured it was Sherry Grady's doing. She'd seen that the two of them were friends and she meant to break it up. She meant to make him trouble any which way, even if she had to make cow eyes at the marshal to do it.

He told himself that had to be her reason. She'd never had any use for lawmen — leastways not while Charlie was working for Harry Wolfe. She sure wouldn't naturally be friendly with Edwards. That notion satisfied him better than the idea that she'd really taken a shine to the marshal.

Dammit, why did she have to be such an ornery woman, and such a handsome one?

Eventually he gave up any hope of Edwards' returning. After he'd bedded his horse, he drifted up Grant Street feeling an empty restlessness, wishing he were somewhere else altogether.

The lights were bright in the Oriental. Laughter and lively music washed through the doorway. Looking at the lights, he told himself he'd probably be walking straight into trouble if he went in there.

He went anyway.

The attention he drew as he stepped into the saloon was sharp-edged with hostility. Townsmen whose faces weren't familiar at all turned to glare at him. Well, that was no surprise. Not after that run-in with Christy on the street. People were bound to think the worst — especially since the shooting affair with Sherry.

He glanced across the faces that turned toward him, thinking that if a jury ever looked at a man that way, he might as well plead guilty and be done with it.

Liz Gerard was in the saloon, at a back table. She was involved in a card game, probably representing the house. He wondered which side of the deck she dealt from. He couldn't spot Steele or Carlisle anywhere in the room, which didn't mean one or the other wouldn't show up. But for the time being, he figured he could have a quiet drink.

As he leaned an elbow on the bar, he asked himself if a quiet drink was what he really wanted. There were other places in town he could have gone to where he'd have had a better chance of peace and quiet. Maybe he'd chosen to come here because he really was hunting trouble. A fist-fight, maybe? A chance to lash out and break something, smash his knuckles into something hard but yielding, like maybe Shorty Steele's face? He had to admit the idea had a kind of appeal. He sure hankered to do something to shatter the taut restlessness that plagued him.

Rudd Kelly was at the far end of the bar, deep in conversation with a couple of customers. He glanced toward Glencannon, broke off his talk, and hurried over. Breathlessly, he said, "You shouldn't have come here."

Something was wrong, Glencannon thought. Yesterday Kelly'd been afraid of him and the implied threat he'd dropped. Some of that fear should still be with the man, unless he knew something now he hadn't known then. Had Christy broken her word and spread it around that he really was Shea Glencannon? And would that particular piece of information have eased the bartender's fears?

"Wait and let Liz get in touch with you," Kelly said, almost pleading.

"About what?"

"You know what."

"I do?"

The bartender nodded. "Wait for Liz."

"All right. Suppose you give me a beer while I wait," Glencannon said, wondering what the man was talking about.

"But —"

"You gonna give me a beer?"

Sighing, Kelly turned to pick up a mug from the shelf. As he drew the drink, his eyes darted to the backbar mirror. He was looking at Liz Gerard's reflection. Glencannon could see it too. She seemed intent on the game, not knowing or caring that he was there.

Kelly put the beer in front of him. Some of it slopped out of the mug. The bartender's hand was shaking. Leaning toward Glencannon, he begged, "Please, you'll ruin everything. Don't do anything until you've talked to Liz."

"Maybe I ought to talk to her right now."

"No! Not in here!"

"Where?"

Kelly didn't know what to say. He scanned the room. Swallowing hard, he suggested, "Outside in front. I'll send her to you."

Nodding, Glencannon picked up the beer and stepped through the doorway. He stood in the half-shadow between the door and the window, thinking as how he'd managed to get a wedge into whatever was going on in this town. A little more pressure and maybe he'd have it wide open. What was that old story about somebody prying the lid off a box and having a faceful of troubles come flying out of it at him?

Liz Gerard came through the batwings. Anxiously she said, "This is the wrong time and place."

"Maybe there ain't gonna be a *right* time and place." He responded, wondering what she was talking about.

She gazed at him in the light spilling from the saloon, waiting as someone went past on the walkway. Then she said, "I know you're Shea."

"You're sure of it?"

She nodded. "You don't look much like your father, except for the eyes. You've got Jake's eyes. We'd thought you were dead, but when I saw you, I knew. . . ."

"Just how much did Christy tell you?"

She looked startled, suddenly distracted

123

from whatever she'd been thinking. "Christy? What's Christy got to do with this?"

"She told you I was Shea. What else did she tell you?"

"Christy didn't tell me. I knew you by your eyes — but, how would Christy know? I've tried to keep her out of this. What's happened? How is she involved?"

The woman was really afraid now, for her daughter's sake, he thought. He felt a surge of sympathy for her. It would be easy to like her . . . if he hadn't suspected her of a part in his father's murder. But Christy hadn't had anything to do with that.

He answered, "She heard Ted Edwards call me by name. She wants Carlisle killed."

"No! Oh, no! Carlisle can't — no, Shea! You've got to go away!"

"Somebody murdered my pa. I want to know who and why."

"Please, Shea," the woman said desperately. "Leave us alone."

He shook his head. "I've got a right here. I've got a right to know what happened."

Someone was coming along the walk. The woman glanced at the figure. She clasped her hands together, twisting the fingers, as she waited for the person to pass on out of earshot. In a harsh whisper she said, "I *can't* talk to you here, now. I'll tell you everything later."

"When?"

"Later — tonight, after the saloon closes. I'll come. Wait in your room."

She sounded sincere. He told himself that she might send Shorty Steele with a gun instead. He didn't quite believe it though. And, hell, he'd be ready in case it did happen. "All right."

Even in the dimness he could see relief flood her face. She gave him a brief attempt at a smile as she wheeled to hurry back into the saloon.

She was honestly frightened, but not of him. Of George Carlisle, he thought. But if that was so, why was it *him* she wanted to hustle out of town?

He finished off the beer, then walked inside to set the mug on the bar.

"There's nothing you can do, Glencannon," Rudd Kelly said softly, leaning toward him. "Except maybe get yourself killed. Why don't you get out of here and leave us alone?"

So Kelly was in on Liz's secrets, he thought. He gave a slow shake of his head.

"If you hang around here, you won't be the only one to get killed," the barkeep persisted. "If not for Liz, then for Christy's

sake. Believe me, he won't stop at anything!"

"Carlisle?" Glencannon asked.

"Steele!" Kelly said, almost gasping. But
it wasn't an answer to the question. He was
looking past Glencannon. In hoarse warning, he added, "Coming this way."

"That's just fine with me." Glencannon
rubbed one hand into the other in antici-
pation. "I've been kinda looking forward —"

"No, please don't!" Kelly grunted. He
jerked back, turning to busy himself with
his bar rag, as Steele stepped up beside
Glencannon.

The little man's face was stiff in an attempt to mask his emotions. Coldly, he
said, "Boss wants to see you."

"Me?" Glencannon grunted, making
himself sound surprised.

"Yeah."

"Maybe I don't want to see him."

"I said the boss wants to see you," Steele
repeated, putting an edge of threat into his
voice.

"Alone in his office, huh?"

"Yeah."

Casually, Glencannon drew the handgun
from his holster. He checked the loads he
already knew were in place, making a show
of it for Steele. Returning the gun to the

holster, he settled it loosely. "All right."

Steele's eyes were narrow with hatred. "Come on," he muttered, heading for the stairs.

The door was closed. Steele knocked and Carlisle's voice answered. Opening the door, Steele stepped back to let Glencannon enter first.

Grinning slightly, Glencannon shook his head.

"Well, come on in," Carlisle snapped impatiently.

Defeated in the small gesture, Steele walked on into the room with Glencannon behind him. There was a rigidness about his spine, as if he expected Glencannon's gun to prod into it any minute. But Glencannon's only move was to sidestep as he entered the room, putting his back to the wall. He stood waiting, studying the man behind the desk.

Carlisle looked like a man completely satisfied with himself, confident that he was master of any situation. Returning Glencannon's gaze, he said, "Some things can be settled as well with gold as with guns."

Glencannon lifted an eyebrow in question.

"You came here for a price, didn't you? You could just as well leave for one. Ride out a richer man, with no harm done. No danger to yourself at all."

Amazed, Glencannon almost laughed. Like Christy, Carlisle had taken him to be a hired gun. But Carlisle figured he was here on business, and wanted to get rid of him before he set in to work.

"How much is she paying you?" the man asked.

"She?"

"Liz Gerard. She's the one who sent for you, isn't she?"

Glencannon shook his head.

That reply didn't suit Carlisle. He had his idea of what was going on, and he wasn't willing to give it up. He thought a moment, then said, "Who was it? The old man?"

"Jake Glencannon?"

It wasn't an answer, but it seemed to satisfy Carlisle as one. It fit his notions. "Well, Jake's dead now. You won't be working for him."

"I guess not," Glencannon agreed.

"You don't have any obligation to a dead man." Carlisle smiled expansively. "Even if you've already been paid, you've got no obligation."

"I wouldn't exactly say that."

The smile was suddenly gone. Carlisle's face was hard and threatening. "Look,

128

mister, Liz is throwing in her hand. If she doesn't, I can promise you she'll be plenty sorry. And anybody who lines himself up on her side will be sorry too."

Steele nodded vigorously in agreement.

"I'm on *my* side," Glencannon said.

Carlisle seemed to like that answer too. He brought back his smile. "Line your own pockets, eh? Devil take the hindmost. Well, you look handy. Maybe you'd like to work for me?"

"Boss!" Steele gasped.

"Shut up!"

"But, boss, he's got — I — boss, get rid of him!"

Carlisle glared the little man into silence. Turning on his smile again, he said to Glencannon, "It might be the final straw I need. It'll break Liz to find the man she's been depending on working for me. How about it?"

"No."

The smile weakened. "Either you'll work for me or you'll leave this town quick."

"You sure of that?" Glencannon asked blandly.

"Yeah!"

He shrugged. "You got anything else to say to me?"

"No!" Anger had begun to flush Carlisle's face.

Glencannon opened the door and stepped out. Grinning to himself, he closed it behind him. Through the panels, he could hear Steele protesting, "But, boss, he's got the watch!"

"That's your damnfool mistake!" Carlisle snapped back. "Take care of it any way you want. Now, get out!"

Glencannon strode quickly away.

Heading for his room, he studied over the things that had happened. It was the fancy timepiece that had Steele so upset. It had been Jake's. Steele must have stolen it, when he killed Jake. He'd sold it to a man he figured for a drifter just passing through. But the drifter and the watch stayed in Broken Crossing and Steele was afraid that the murder would catch up with him.

He felt certain Steele had killed Jake at Carlisle's order. But he couldn't prove it. Well, maybe Liz Gerard could. At the least, she could answer some of the questions that were plaguing him.

Inside the room, he stretched out on the bed. With his hands under his head, he stared at the ceiling, waiting for her to come.

Slowly, but inevitably, his thoughts turned to Sherry Grady. She seemed bound and determined to lift his scalp. It seemed like she was putting all of her mind and her life to that one goal. How could a man like Charlie have been that important to her? Why couldn't she see and understand that the way Charlie'd been going he was due to be gunned down by someone? Why hadn't she tried to get him away from Harry Wolfe and his kind if he meant so much to her?

He wondered if maybe she had tried — and failed. That might be a part of the way she felt now. She hadn't been able to keep Charlie alive, so now she felt bound to revenge his death.

But why Charlie Grady? How did a man go about making a girl like Sherry care that much about him? And how could a man keep a girl like Sherry from lifting his scalp, without hurting her in any way?

That was the question he *had* to find an answer for.

Chapter 10

A hard pounding at the door woke Glencannon suddenly. As he blinked open his eyes, he realized it was morning. He'd fallen asleep waiting for Liz Gerard. And that sure wasn't her hammering at his door.

Grimacing at the brightness of the sunlight that speared through the window, he hollered, "What's all the ruckus?"

"Shea, open up!" It was Ted Edwards' voice that answered. And he sounded plenty excited about something.

Another murder, Glencannon wondered, getting to his feet. He jerked back the bolt and swung open the door.

Edwards had a revolver in his hand. It pointed at Glencannon's chest.

"Huh?" Glencannon took a step back and to the side. But the muzzle of the gun followed him. The tension began to twist itself in his gut. "What's the matter, Ted?"

"You're under arrest." Edwards' voice

was unnaturally loud. His hand was almost trembling.

"For anything in particular?" Glen-cannon took another backstep as he tugged the Bull sack out of his vest pocket. He looked at his own hands as he built himself a cigarette. But he was aware of the people who'd begun to crowd into the hallway, watching and listening.

Edwards was aware of them too. Seeming embarrassed, he moved on into the room and closed the door behind him. Patting his shirt pocket with his left hand, he said, "I got a telegram here."

"Got a match?"

"No! Dammit, Shea, this is serious. I got a telegram here from the sheriff of Gwinnett County in Arizona."

"From old Harry Wolfe?" Glencannon showed signs of interest.

"He's got a warrant for your arrest," Edwards said.

"I reckon I got a match here somewhere," Glencannon mumbled, running his hands over his pockets.

"I'm *serious*," Edwards repeated. "I got to arrest you."

"What for?"

"Murder."

"On a warrant from Harry Wolfe?"

The marshal nodded. "He's sending a couple of deputies with the warrant. He's telegraphed me for official cooperation and I got to hold you."

Glencannon glanced at the gun. "If *I* don't cooperate with you, you gonna shoot me?"

"Hell," Edwards muttered in frustration. He wasn't sure what he'd do if Glencannon made trouble for him. But he had his duty. "I don't *want* to, Shea, but if I *have* to . . ." Letting the words trail off, he silently implored Glencannon to cooperate.

Glencannon found the matches. Indolently, he lit the cigarette, then flipped the dead match toward the spittoon. Edwards glanced at it. And Glencannon moved.

His arm rammed across the marshal's as he spun. It knocked the gun aside. The hammer snapped down and lead slammed into the wall, spattering plaster. Beyond the closed door somebody gave a startled shout.

How long would it take one of those people in the hall to work up courage and open the door? Glencannon wondered as he clamped a hand on Edwards' wrist. He didn't want to hurt the marshal, but he had to make this quick. And, dammit, he was sick of being pushed around in this town.

"Shea!" Edwards shouted in surprised protest. His free hand clawed at the fingers locked onto his wrist. But he couldn't loosen the grip that way. And Glencannon was twisting hard. His arm was being forced back, his grip on the gun loosened.

Edwards jerked back the free hand and drove his knuckles toward Glencannon's side.

The fist struck hard — and square into the healing wound. Pain jarred like the strike of lightning against Glencannon's ribs. It drove the breath — and strength — out of him. As he staggered back, Edwards jerked free of his grip.

The pain the marshal felt wasn't physical. He hurt with frustration. He was a lawman, doing his job the best he could. But everybody fought him. Even a friend like Shea Glencannon fought him. He couldn't take any more of it. The animal urge to fight back overwhelmed him.

Through a sudden haze, Glencannon saw Edwards' face twist with fury. The marshal wasn't leveling the gun now, but raising it, swinging it wildly, like a club.

Glencannon threw up both hands. He caught the blow against his arm. But Edwards was swinging again.

"Hold on, Ted!" he hollered, trying to

grab the flailing revolver. His hand wrapped around the cylinder but he couldn't stop the momentum of the swing. The gun slammed his own knuckles into his face.

Half-stunned, he fell back against the wall. He couldn't see through the red pain, or hold up a hand to defend himself. It was all he could do to keep to his feet. Hoarsely, he gasped, "Ted!"

He expected another slashing blow of the gun. But it didn't come. And as the first flood of pain in his face eased, he made out the marshal's blurred figure standing back from him. There were other figures too. People jammed in the now-open doorway, staring and murmuring among themselves.

Motionless, Edwards stood with the gun hanging limply at his side. Now that the flare of anger had faded, he was aghast at his own ferocity. Gazing at the blood that smeared Glencannon's face, he asked tentatively, "Shea, you all right?"

"Yeah, I guess so." Glencannon lifted a hand to dab at the blood. He winced at his own touch and added, "I think you busted my nose."

"Why the hell didn't you give in and come along peaceable?" Edwards said.

Without answering, Glencannon turned to the washstand. He dipped a corner of the towel in the pitcher and wiped at his face. He was still weak almost to the point of shaking and the tension in his belly was hard-knotted. Drawing deep breaths through his mouth, he tried to ease it. Strength began to seep slowly back. He tested his nose with his fingertips and decided it wasn't broken. But it was plenty sore. So was his side where Edwards had hammered a fist into the healing wound. Leaning a hand on the washstand, he faced the marshal again. "You sure fight dirty."

Edwards wasn't sure whether to be embarrassed or angry again. The emotions mixed in him. "I'm the law here," he said defensively. "Come on, Shea, I got to lock you up till those deputies get here."

"For shooting Charlie Grady?"

"Yeah."

Sighing, Glencannon started for the door. The crowd of watchers opened a path for him. And Edwards followed behind, as if herding him. As he came to the stairs, he saw Sherry Grady.

She stood at the bottom of the staircase, looking up expectantly. *So* this *was her hole card,* he thought. *She'd sent word to*

Harry Wolfe. She was the one who'd asked for the warrant.

As he neared her, she met his eyes with a smile of triumph. "They're coming for you, Glencannon. They'll hang you."

"You reckon they will?" he said levelly. "Harry's sending a couple of deputies for me, is he? They won't hang me, Sherry. I won't live to be hanged."

She looked like she didn't understand. He wondered if maybe she really didn't. "They won't take me back on the stage," he told her. "We'll pack out on horseback, overland. You watch and see. And when I get to Gwinnett, it'll be over my saddle with a couple of bullets in my back. They'll say as how I tried to escape and they had to shoot me down. But you'll know it was plain, simple murder, won't you, Sherry?"

The notion seemed to shock her. But she snapped at him, "Like you murdered Charlie!"

"I didn't shoot Charlie in the back. And *he* had a gun in his hand."

"Leave her alone, Glencannon," Edwards said harshly. "Haven't you hurt her enough already?"

Glancing over his shoulder, Glencannon started to protest. But he saw that cow-eyed look on the marshal's face and he knew it was no use arguing. When he turned back, Sherry was hurrying away.

She had to push through the people standing at the doorway, gaping. Edwards shouted at them, "You folks, get on back where you belong! This ain't no medicine show!"

"Ain't it?" Glencannon muttered to himself as he moved on.

All three jail cells were empty. Glencannon chose for himself. He picked the one where they'd found the corpse that had been buried under his name. He stood gazing at the dark stain set fast into the planks of the floor as Edwards slammed the barred door shut behind him.

Sighing, he stretched out on the cot with his hands under his head. This was one hell of a mess. And he had to figure a way out of it before those deputies from Harry Wolfe arrived or he'd *never* get out. Not alive, he wouldn't.

Edwards had gone back into the office, closing the solid oak door between it and the cells. Was he still in the office, Glencannon wondered, or was he off chasing after Sherry Grady? Seemed like there wasn't anything that could mess up a man's thinking — or his life — the way a woman could. Sherry had the marshal so twisted up now that he couldn't see straight. And she had *him* set up like a bottle on a stump.

Gazing at the small high window, he envisioned the snout of a shotgun poked between the bars. The man who'd been in the cell must have been looking at the gun when it went off. It had caught him full in the face. From the position they'd found the body in, he'd have been standing about there. Glencannon looked down at the floor and the bloodstain.

It was all wrong, he thought with a sudden excitement. To thrust a gun muzzle through the window, someone outside would have had to stand on something as high as the rain barrel. The floor in here wasn't much above ground level. To hit a man standing on the floor, the gun would have pointed down at a fairly sharp angle. And shot spreads. A lot of it would have gone past the victim. There should have been lead embedded in the floor of the cell. But there wasn't.

He clambered off the cot to hunker and study the planks. Not a trace of lead, not a splinter, not a mark where a piece of shot might have hit and ricocheted. Nothing under the cot either, except a lot of dust mice. And a feather.

He picked it up and turned it between his fingers. Dominicker, same as the ones he'd found in the yard, and not any pillow feather either. This was a wing quill. And there were dark splotches on it. Blood — like the blood that stained the floor.

Rising to his feet, he hollered, "Ted!"

He had to shout three times before the oak door finally opened and the marshal looked in.

"What is it?" Edwards growled.

Glencannon held up the feather. "Look at this."

"So?"

Dammit, couldn't Edwards see anything? he thought with angry impatience. He snapped, "Are you so het up over Sherry Grady that you've lost interest in the murders around here?"

"You leave Sherry out of this!"

"Oh, hell, Ted! Look, there's been two men murdered in this town already. Maybe more. You care about it or not?"

"What do you mean maybe more'n two?" Edwards answered sullenly. "And what the devil's a chicken feather got to do with it?"

"I mean I got a notion the man we buried wasn't the same one who claimed to be me. You had one man locked up in

141

this cell — but you found a different man dead in it."

"Huh?" Edwards grunted in puzzlement.

"The doctor must have looked over the body when he laid it out," Glencannon said. "Let's us go have a talk with him."

"Oh, no! *You* ain't going anywhere."

"Then fetch the doctor over here and we'll talk."

The marshal eyed him skeptically. "You're trying to pull some kind of trick on me, ain't you, Shea?"

"No!" he snapped back.

Edwards shook his head in disbelief.

"Dammit, Ted, I'm telling you the truth."

"I dunno. Shea, it's been a long time since we were kids together. I don't know you no more. Don't know what to expect from you. Not after the way you jumped me this morning."

"What do you expect? You come busting into my room waving a gun at me. What'd you expect me to do?"

He frowned as he thought about it.

"Look here, Ted," Glencannon continued, "Sherry's told you a lot of things the way *she* sees them. But ain't it possible she's looking at it all kinda one-sided? Yeah, I shot her husband. I'll own to that. But you reckon she's gonna admit her husband was a low-down thief and murderer by trade and that he damn near killed me at the same time?"

"She wouldn't lie to me!" Edwards protested.

"Maybe not on purpose. But maybe she don't know she's lying. Maybe she hasn't admitted to herself what kind Charlie really was."

Edwards gazed at the floor as he considered. He shifted his weight from one foot to the other and shook his head uncertainly.

Taking a deep breath, Glencannon tried again. "Ted, those deputies Wolfe's sending after me ain't gonna get here for maybe a week. You intend to keep me prisoner till then. All right, I ain't asking you to let me go. But I want to get my pa's murder cleared up. Why the devil can't you and me make peace with each other and try to work it out together? All I'm asking you to do is fetch that doctor over here so I can talk to him."

"All right," the marshal sighed. "If he's back in town, I'll bring him over."

143

Chapter 11

Glencannon stretched out on the cot to wait. He lay gazing at the window as time dragged slowly past. Finally he heard sounds from the office, and the big oak door swung open.

Edwards stood in the doorway. He still looked doubtful as he said, "The doctor ain't back down from the mountains yet."

Glencannon looked past him at Sherry Grady. She was standing at the marshal's side with her hand wrapped tightly in his. *Come to gloat?* The thought set the anger burning in him again. His eyes on hers, he said, "Come on in. We can hold a celebration."

"Celebrating what?" Edwards asked suspiciously.

"My funeral. She promised to dance on my coffin. Maybe if I ask her real nice, she'll give a demonstration before she nails the lid shut."

"You murdered my husband!" She

shouted it at him as if it were the only important thing in the world to her.

He told himself that shouting back wasn't going to do any good. It'd just make Ted Edwards madder, and he sure didn't want that. With effort, he kept his voice calm. "I'll own I went after Charlie with the intent of killing him. But he had his gun and he had his chance. He come near to killing me. I can prove that. And I'd never have gone after him if he hadn't shot down J.J. the way he did."

She started to spit some answer at him, but Edwards stopped her. The marshal looked caught, torn with uncertainty. "Shea," he asked, "if you're so sure you can prove it was a fair fight, how come you're afraid to stand trial for it?"

"I ain't afraid of a trial. I just don't like the idea of being slaughtered like a beef at the knackers. Ted, you don't know this Sheriff Harry Wolfe and his bunch. Once they get hold of me, they'll never let me come to trial."

"Why not?"

It was a chance to speak his piece. Glencannon grabbed at it. "There are a lot of folk in Gwinnett who are pretty well fed up with Harry and his ways. He's afraid some one of 'em just might find himself

145

nerve enough to get up on the witness stand and speak his mind. Harry's got a tight rein on Gwinnett, but he ain't all-powerful, and if word of his ways was to get to the governor . . ."

"You're afraid because Harry'll hang you," Sherry interrupted. "Charlie was one of Harry's men and Harry don't put up with anybody killing his men. Harry takes care of them and they take care of him. None of those fat little storekeepers would ever have the guts to go against Harry Wolfe!"

"Those fat little storekeepers have had a gizzardful of Harry. They're ready to stand up against him right now. They just ain't got the ways to do it. What they need is somebody to back their hand and stand up with 'em. They *sent* for J.J. and if he hadn't been murdered —"

"*Sent* for him?" She sounded like it was a lot more than she could swallow.

Glencannon nodded.

"What are you talking about?" Edwards asked.

"J. J. McKibbin and the people of Gwinnett, Arizona," Glencannon told him. "What did *she* say about it?"

He looked even more confused now. He spoke hesitantly, as if he were embarrassed by what he was saying. "She told me you and this J. J. McKibbin showed up in Gwinnett and challenged the elected peace officers. She said McKibbin bulled his way into the marshal's job and tried to take over running the town and that you backed him up with a gun. She got me to thinking as how, well — the way you've been grabbing at the reins around here — she got me to thinking you meant to try the same thing here in Broken Crossing."

Did she really believe that? Glencannon asked himself. As he considered it, he built himself a cigarette. He could feel Sherry's intense gaze. And Edwards' puzzlement. Did Ted really believe he'd try something like that? It made a kind of sense, he supposed. But it sure wasn't true.

He lit the cigarette and said slowly, "Ted, if you got word of *me* this far up-country, you sure must have heard of J. J. McKibbin."

"A little. But there wasn't anybody around here talking his name up the way your pa did yours."

"Yeah." Glencannon wondered just what his father had been saying about him. But the important thing right now was to convince the marshal that the things Sherry Grady had said were lies, or at least mistakes. "J. J. McKibbin was a lawman clear through to the bone," he said. "He was a U.S. Deputy Marshal for a while and for a couple of years he was an investigator for Wells Fargo. After that — well, you've heard of Red Branch in Kansas?"

Edwards nodded.

"That was a rough town. It kinked up in the morning and got worse as the day went on. There were folks in the town who knew about J.J. and they sent for him. He took hold of Red Branch and gentled it down till it fair ate out of his hand without baring its teeth. He made it tame enough for ladies and small children. Then he got an election held for new peace officers and he moved on out. If J.J. had wanted himself a town to run, he could have had Red Branch then and there. But that wasn't what he wanted."

Sherry was still staring at him with that cold hatred. But she didn't interrupt. She was listening.

"What about Gwinnett?" Edwards asked.

"This sheriff Harry Wolfe has Gwinnett County flat under his thumb. There's silver in the county and Harry gets his share without ever putting a spade to the ground. He runs the town wide open. Him and his men help themselves to just about anything they fancy. But there's a lot of decent folk in the town who've been fed up with him for a long time. They haven't been able to vote him out because his men handle the elections, and by themselves, they ain't quite got the nerve to buck up to him. So they got together and formed a committee . . ."

"Vigilantes?" the marshal grunted.

Glencannon shook his head. "No, more of a town council. They said they were lawbiding folk and didn't hold with the vigilante kind of thing. I think that mostly they were just plain too scared to try it, though. Vigilantes have to have themselves a strong leader. These people didn't. So they sent for J.J. and asked him to come and tame Harry Wolfe for them. Said they wanted it all done real legal."

The skepticism had faded in Edwards. He muttered, "All right. But how'd *you* get into it?"

"I'd known J.J. for a while back when we were both working for Wells Fargo. We run into each other when he was on his way to Gwinnett. He asked me if I'd like to ride along. He knew the kind that Harry is, and he wanted somebody to cover his back." Glencannon fished the deputy's badge out of his pocket and shoved it through the

149

bars. Bitterly, he added, "I reckon I didn't do a very good job of it."

Edwards looked at the star with a nod. He knew Glencannon had been carrying one in Gwinnett. He just didn't know what it was worth. Sherry'd made it out to be a shield for corruption. Glencannon made it sound like something he'd respected. Thoughtfully, he asked Glencannon, "What happened?"

"J.J. set out to do things the way the townfolk wanted, all nice and legal. But every time he'd make a move, Harry'd stall him in some damned way. It ain't easy to fight a man by the rules when he's happy to use every dirty trick there is. It came to the point where we knew we couldn't lick him by ourselves, so J.J. started setting up a case against him, figuring to get enough evidence to interest the territorial governor. He got a few folk convinced and they promised to stand up and speak out. He was about ready to head for Tucson, but before he could leave, he got shot down . . ." Glencannon turned toward Sherry. She was watching him, her eyes steady, her face tensely expressionless.

". . . by Charlie Grady," he added. He licked his thumb, pinched out the cigarette and tossed it on the floor.

150

Edwards seemed to be considering the story with interest and even a glimmer of belief. He glanced at Sherry, then looked to Glencannon again. "So you went gunning for Grady?"

"Yeah."

"If McKibbin had evidence, why didn't *you* take it to the governor, the same way he'd been planning to?"

"Wolfe buffaloed that idea good. When J.J. got shot down, it scared the folks who'd intended to fight along with us. The witnesses all went scurrying for their holes. Suddenly nobody in town knew anything. Except a bunch of Harry's men. They claimed they'd seen the shooting. Stood up at the inquest and testified that J.J.'d been bulling around in a poker game. Said he'd gone for his gun when Charlie called him down for a dirty deal, and that Charlie'd outdrawn him. Said Charlie shot in self-defense." He snorted in disgust. "There'd been witnesses to what really happened, but there wasn't a one of 'em to stand up and speak out when the time came."

"What makes you think you know what really happened?" Sherry demanded. "Did *you* see it?"

"No," he admitted. "But one of those witnesses showed himself a mite. He came

151

sneaking to me, scared sick, but game to tell me how Charlie'd just walked into the room with a gun in his hand and shot down J.J. without a word to warn him."

"That's a lie!" she snapped. "Charlie would never have done a thing like that!"

"Wouldn't he? You know how much Charlie liked being one of Harry's men. You know how much he liked having money in his pockets — how he liked hanging around the saloon showing off what a big man he was. To keep that, he'd have done anything Harry told him to do."

She spun to face Edwards. "It's a lie! It's all a lie! He murdered Charlie!"

"If anybody *murdered* Charlie," Glencannon said, working hard to keep his voice soft and level, "it was Harry Wolfe, by sending him to do a killing like that. You shouldn't have let Charlie do it, Sherry. You should never have let him get in that deep with Harry in the first place."

"A lie!" She repeated desperately. Her voice broke. She pressed her face into Edwards' shoulder, catching at her breath as if she were about to cry. Almost inaudibly, she said, "I tried."

The marshal took her arms. "Sherry, look at me."

Reluctantly, she raised her head. As her

eyes met his, he asked her, "Is Shea telling me the truth?"

For an instant she just stared at him. With a sudden wrench of her shoulders, she pulled free of his hands. "Damn you! All of you with your tin stars! That sets you above everybody else, doesn't it? That tin star! You can do what you want and take what you want and to hell with everybody else. You'd take a poor sweet boy like Charlie and make a killer out of him!" She jerked her head toward Glencannon. "He killed Charlie just because he wanted me. Now you'll kill him for the same reason, won't you! You — you — !" Choking on her own words, tears streaming down her face, she turned away from Edwards and ran through the door.

Aghast, he shouted after her as he followed. "Sherry!"

They were both gone from Glencannon's sight. He stood with his hands wrapped around the bars, looking at the empty doorway. He knew he'd hurt her bad. He'd spread the truth out in front of her and made her look at it, face on.

She hadn't been willing to see — to admit to herself — what her husband had been and why he'd died. And she still didn't see it clearly or understand it all.

But he'd forced her to look at it.

She held herself to blame for Charlie's death, he thought. She felt that somehow she'd failed her husband because she hadn't managed to turn him off the path that led him to his death. She'd even set out to revenge him by doing a killing herself.

But if she admitted to herself that Charlie had been wrong, then she had to admit her attempt to avenge him was wrong, too.

It was a rotten, stinking mess, Glencannon thought. No matter what way he looked at it — no matter how it all worked out — it was still a rotten, stinking mess.

Chapter 12

Daylight was waning when Edwards finally came back. This time he had Doc Palmer with him.

Looking sheepishly apologetic, he began, "Shea, I kinda . . . Sherry — she . . ." He couldn't quite say what it was that he had on his mind. Instead, he said, "I brought the doc as quick as I could."

Glencannon read the meaning in the few stammered words. The marshal had accepted his side of the Gwinnett business. That realization flooded him with a sense of relief. But it didn't solve any problems, he told himself. He nodded greeting to the doctor.

Palmer looked weary. His eyes were red-rimmed and his clothes dun with road dust. But there was a lively curiosity in his face. "So you're Shea Glencannon," he said.

"It kinda looks that way," Glencannon answered.

"What's Ted got you jailed for? That young lady bring charges against you after all?"

He nodded.

The doctor looked a little surprised. "I thought even Ted agreed that shooting was in self-defense."

"Different shooting," Glencannon told him.

"Oh? Serious?"

"Maybe hanging serious."

"Well, I've lost more than one promising patient on the end of a rope," Palmer said with a slight shrug. But he looked as if he didn't really expect to lose this one that way. There was a trace of amusement in his eyes. He seemed to be anticipating something he expected to enjoy. He went on, "Ted says you're hellbent to talk to me about something but you won't tell him what. He dragged me off the minute I got back to town. I hope it's worth the trouble."

"I want to ask you about that corpse we put away yesterday. Did you look it over good before you nailed it in the box?"

Palmer nodded. The corners of his mouth seemed to be trying to twist into a grin, but he struggled to keep his face innocently straight.

He knows all right, Glencannon thought.

He asked, "You notice anything unusual about it?"

Puzzlement was slashed across Edwards' face. But the doctor nodded and gave up fighting the grin. "You mean the fact that the man had been dead at least a day, maybe longer, before I got possession of the body? Or the fact that it wasn't the shotgun blast that killed him?"

"What the devil . . . ?" Edwards grunted like he'd been hit in the stomach. "What are you talking about?"

"Tell him," Glencannon said. He'd discovered the doctor knew more about this than he did.

"Did you notice how limp the body was?" Palmer asked the marshal.

"That's natural, ain't it? A man stays limp a while after he's killed, don't he?"

"Sometimes. Sometimes rigor mortis sets in a few minutes after death and is gone in a few hours. Sometimes it doesn't set in until hours after death and lasts for days. Depends on the weather, the physical condition of the deceased, and the cause of death. Your corpse had been in bad shape. Rigor mortis came and went quickly. It was past when you called me to pick up the body. When I realized that, I got curious and took the liberty of examining his lights." The doctor glanced knowingly at Glencannon. "There wasn't much sign of organic putrefaction yet. That meant he hadn't been dead more than three or four days — not in this heat. But there was enough to indicate he'd been dead around twenty-four hours."

Edwards pondered that. Indignantly, he said, "Why didn't you tell me about this? I'm marshal here."

"I meant to but I got called off for that appendix up in the mountains and never got the opportunity."

"What did he die from?" Glencannon asked.

"Ruptured blood vessel. He was thoroughly dead from natural causes before his face was mutilated by the shotgun blast."

"That's why you never heard a shotgun in the backyard that night, Doc. Nobody fired one off."

"I don't get it!" Edwards snapped, angered by his sense of being left out, and completely puzzled.

"The way it looks to me," Glencannon told him, "somebody wanted to break that imitation Shea Glencannon out of your jail. He found this drifter already dead and it gave him an idea. He slipped you knockout drops and took the face off the corpse with a shotgun. He hauled the body over here and the fake Glencannon switched clothes with it. They butchered a chicken — a dominicker — here to make fresh bloodstains. Then they lit out, brushing over their tracks so nobody'd be able to tell there was two of 'em."

Palmer was nodding and grinning. It struck Glencannon that he looked like a spectator at a play who'd guessed how it was going to work out and was delighted at seeing it go the way he'd expected. Now he was anticipating the next act.

Edwards still didn't have it figured though. He asked, "Why would they go to all that trouble?"

"It left you thinking the man you'd had in jail on a murder charge was dead. You'd be looking for his killer instead of him. He'd get away clean without the law on his tail," Glencannon answered.

The marshal gazed at the floor, frowning thoughtfully. Still angry, and a little bewildered, he grunted, "What else you know about all this that I don't?"

"Not much. But I got some ideas."

"For instance?"

"For instance, you take my parole and we can clean up this whole business."

"I can't do that."

"Why not? You know I ain't been lying about Charlie Grady's death."

"I know. But I can't take your parole."

"Are you still so calf-eyed about Sherry that you can't see straight?" Glencannon snapped.

"No! Dammit, Shea, murder is a serious charge," the marshal answered. "Whatever you say about this Harry Wolfe, he's still the lawful sheriff in Gwinnett. I got his official request for cooperation. If I was to take your parole and then you crossed me and lit out . . . I couldn't much blame you — but I can't take no chance on your doing it."

"You got my word, Ted."

"I ain't taking your word!"

Glencannon sighed wearily. It looked like talk wasn't going to do any good. J.J. had always said to use words first: never use force until you'd run out of words and proved they wouldn't work. Well, he'd tried, Glencannon told himself. But now he was out of words. It looked like he'd have to handle this thing his own way. "All right, if you don't *want* my help . . ."

"Looks to me like you both need each other's help," Doc Palmer put in.

"But I can't let him out of jail," Edwards protested.

"You got your mind made up," Glencannon said, as if he were giving in.

Edwards yielded a little then. Apologetically, he said, "It's what I got to do."

"All right." Fingering in a pocket, Glencannon found the chicken feathers. They'd do. He held them up. "Then take a look at these."

"Why?"

"Take a look at them," he repeated, thrusting them out a little ways between the bars of the cell.

Edwards leaned forward to squint curiously at them.

"Take 'em," Glencannon grunted. He gave them a shake. "Take 'em and take a good look at 'em."

Stepping toward him, Edwards reached for the feathers.

Dropping them, Glencannon clamped his hand around the marshal's wrist. He threw his weight back, yanking Edwards off balance, pulling his arm through the bars.

"Hey!" Edwards shouted, struggling against him. But Glencannon twisted at the arm, holding the marshal cramped against the bars. With his free hand, he jerked the revolver out of Edwards' holster. As he rammed the muzzle of it into Ed-

161

wards' back, he eased his grip on the arm slightly.

"Hey! Dammit, Shea!"

"Easy, Ted," Glencannon said softly. He looked toward Palmer.

The doctor stood motionless, watching with amusement like a spectator again. He asked, "Now what, Glencannon?"

"Fetch the keys to this cell. Unless you want me to make you a patient out of Ted here."

"I don't think he'd approve of that."

"Damn right I don't!" Edwards grunted through his teeth. Glencannon still had enough pressure on his arm for it to hurt.

"We can do this the easy way or the hard way," Glencannon said. "If I set this gun to the lock, I can blast it apart. But before I take the gun out of your back, Ted, I'll break your arm. So either you can accept my parole and we can work this whole business out together, or else you get a busted arm and a jailbreak both and maybe we end up shooting at each other. You take your choice." With that, he gave Edwards' arm a little more twist.

Painfully, the marshal asked, "You'll swear me an oath, Shea?"

"Yeah."

"*I* think he's a man of his word," the doctor put in.

Edwards yielded with reluctance. "All right, Doc, fetch him the keys."

It wasn't until Palmer'd brought them from the office and unlocked the cell door that Glencannon loosed his grip on the marshal's arm. He headed into the office, with Edwards and Palmer following wordlessly.

"Ted, what'd you do with my gun?" he asked.

Edwards shook his head. "You gave me your oath."

"I know. I ain't quitting. I'll worry about Harry Wolfe when the time comes. But right now, you and me got business at the Oriental. You gonna give me back my gun, or do I have to use yours?" Glencannon gestured with the revolver he held.

Reluctantly, Edwards pulled the gunbelt out of a desk drawer. Glencannon gave him back his own gun then, and picked up the belt to buckle it on.

Bootheels thudded loud on the planks just outside the office door.

Slapping the buckle closed, Glencannon jerked out his Colt as the door was flung open.

The teamster he'd fought in the saloon

stood framed in the doorway. Finding himself staring into a gun barrel, the man groaned, "Oh Lord!"

"Come in here and close that door behind you," Glencannon ordered.

The teamster stepped in. He looked to Edwards for an instant, but his eyes returned to the revolver. There was terror in them. "Marshal," he stammered, "I — I —" His voice trailed off.

"You going to shoot him?" Palmer asked, obviously more amused than worried.

Glencannon hefted the gun. He grinned slightly. "Maybe not."

The teamster swallowed hard and shuffled his feet. He had to swallow a second time before he'd worked up enough voice to talk. "I — I didn't have no part in it! I come here to tell you about it, didn't I?"

"About what?"

"Carlisle and Steele and that Preston feller." He paused to swallow again.

"What about them?" Glencannon prodded.

"I know I ain't no lily, mister, but stealing wimmen — that's too raw for me!"

With a sudden chill along his spine, Glencannon demanded, "What are you talking about?"

"They took off that Christy Gerard girl. Stole her. I didn't have no part in it. I swear I didn't!" His eyes darted from Glencannon to Edwards and back, as if he couldn't figure out which of them was in authority. Edwards wore the star, but Glencannon had the gun. Apparently he couldn't decide. He turned toward the doctor instead, and protested, "I didn't have no part in it!"

"Talk and make sense," Glencannon said. "What's happened?"

"I ain't no friend of Steele's. I just done him a favor now and then for likker money. That's all! They didn't tell me nothing. All I know's what I seen and heard. They took the girl off up to old man Firth's place in the hills. They're holding her there. They done it to scare her ma. That's all I know. I don't hold none with stealing wimmen."

"Why the devil would they do that?" Edwards grunted.

"Liz ain't been going along with Carlisle of her own will," Glencannon told him. "He's been forcing her into it. Looks like now he's trying to force her into something more. Maybe he ain't happy just running the saloon and all. Maybe he wants to own them, too."

Edwards nodded agreement. But the

doctor said, "I've been out of town. You want to explain this to me?"

"When Ted here up and arrested me, word got around that I was Shea Glencannon. I think maybe that spooked Carlisle. He knows I got a legal claim on my pa's share of the business. He wants to wrap up Liz's share before I can team up with her and the two of us cut him out. Least that's the way it looks to me."

"But you might get hanged," Edwards said.

"And I might not," Glencannon answered. "We can't waste all night standing here discussing it. You know where this Firth place is?"

"Sure, it's up in the mountains a ways, over toward —"

Glencannon cut him off and turned to the teamster. "Who took her?"

"Steele and Preston. But old man Firth'll be up there too."

"All right. Ted, I think you'd better ride up there and fetch her back before anything can happen. Doc, can you ride along with him? Take your doctoring bag, just in case."

Palmer nodded, understanding. "I'll take my gun, too."

"Then get going."

"Ain't you coming?" Edwards asked.

"I got something else to take care of."

"What?"

"Liz Gerard."

"Look, Shea, you ride out with us after Christy. Then we can all look up Carlisle together."

"No. Carlisle must be nervous already. If he finds out you've gone after Christy, there's no telling what he'll do. I got to find him and make sure he doesn't do anything."

"He's right," Palmer said.

Edwards nodded agreement. He and the doctor hurried out to collect their horses.

Glencannon turned to the teamster. "You get moving."

"Where?"

"Into a cell. I think I'd better lock you up for the time being."

"You can't lock me up," the man protested. "I ain't broke no law in this town."

"That's all right," Glencannon answered him. "I ain't a lawman in this town."

Chapter 13

The evening crowd had gathered in the Oriental when Glencannon walked in. He paused to scan the room. Carlisle wasn't there. Neither was Liz. But Rudd Kelly was behind the bar, staring at him in a kind of horrified bewilderment.

He stepped up and asked for a drink.

Moving automatically, Kelly gathered a bottle and a glass. His eyes stayed on Glencannon as he did it. He said, "But you were arrested."

Glencannon nodded and asked, "Where's Liz?"

"No," Kelly said. "They've stole Christy. They'll hurt her. You stay out of it."

"Christy's all right. The marshal and Doc Palmer have gone to get her. Where's Liz?"

As he slowly poured the drink, the bartender thought it over. With uncertain relief in his face, he asked, "You're sure she'll be all right?"

Glencannon nodded again. "It's Liz I'm worrying about now. Is Carlisle gonna leave her be once he gets what he wants? Or is he gonna kill her the way he did Jake?"

"She's upstairs," Kelly told him. "Her and Carlisle and a lawyer name of Hartford. They — they're making out the papers."

"What kind of papers?"

"Carlisle's buying the business from her."

"Only she don't want to sell it? So he's threatened Christy to force her to it?"

"Yeah, only — only —"

"Maybe I'd better go and tell her she doesn't have to sell if she doesn't want to." Glencannon downed the drink, then leaned toward the bartender and said softly, "Kelly, if Steele or any of Carlisle's other friends happen to show up while I'm here, you reckon you could hold 'em off with that Greener of yours?"

Reaching under the bar to finger the shotgun, the barkeep nodded. But his eyes were doubtful.

Glencannon didn't like it. He'd backed Kelly down once himself. And how could he trust the bartender to cover his back if Kelly didn't trust himself? But it was the chance he'd have to take. "Don't let any-body go up those stairs," he said.

"Right." Kelly tried to put confidence into his voice, but he didn't quite succeed.

Glencannon climbed the staircase with a feeling a little like a man must have mounting a gallows. The office door was closed. He rapped sharply.

From inside, a voice snapped impatiently, "What is it?"

Glencannon just knocked again, harder this time. The voice called again, but he gave it no answer.

Finally the door jerked open. A pair of squinting blue eyes peered at him from a face like a pale prune with sidewhiskers. He figured this was the lawyer. Shoving past the man, he forced his way into the office.

Carlisle rose from the deep swivel chair behind the desk. Liz Gerard sat stiffly in a straight chair at its side. Her eyes widened at Glencannon, and her hand rose to cover her mouth. There was terror in her face.

Carlisle only hesitated for an instant. With a slow, confident smile, he said, "I thought you were in jail."

"Is that why you didn't invite me to this gathering?" Glencannon glanced at the papers spread over the desk. "I decided to come anyway, seeing as how this business you're messing with is half mine."

"What do you mean by that?"

"You know I'm Jake's son. I figure I'll take over where he left off."

"Shea . . ." Liz Gerard began. It was a small, frightened protest.

He spoke to her, but his attention was full on Carlisle. "The marshal's bringing Christy down from the Firth place now. I think maybe you and I'd better amble over to his office and wait for him there."

Surprise flashed across Carlisle's face, but it was gone as quickly as it had come. Still completely composed and self-assured, he gave Liz a smile that could only have been meant as a threat.

"Shea, I *can't*," she said.

There was more to it than just the danger to Christy, he thought. Carlisle had some other strong hold over her. He told her, "Liz, you've got to either play your hand or give up the game. You can't go on stalling him forever and you know it."

"What's he talking about?" the lawyer asked cautiously. But Carlisle quieted him with the gesture of a hand.

"You coming, Liz?" Glencannon asked.

She gazed at him a moment more, then slowly rose from the chair.

"I can't go on running," she said. "If trying to protect myself means putting Christy in danger . . . Shea, I'll tell the marshal everything. Steele murdered your father at Carlisle's order. I can prove —"

The sudden roar of a gunshot overrode her words. Something kicked Glencannon in the gut. It slung him back hard, smashing the breath out of him.

He staggered, leaning against the wall. His hand was on the butt of the Colt, jerking at it. But the hand didn't feel like his own. His thoughts seemed torn loose of his body, jumbled and uncertain. He was aware of the pain, of the hard struggle for breath, but even they didn't seem real.

The Colt was free of the holster and rising to point toward Carlisle. It seemed an uncommon heavy weight. The hammer under his thumb felt too stiff to ever be moved.

Hazily, he saw the over-under sleeve gun that Carlisle was holding. A thin twist of smoke rose from one barrel.

As he saw it, Glencannon knew what had happened. When Liz spoke, he'd turned to her. For a moment he'd let himself be distracted from Carlisle. And in that moment, Carlisle had snapped out the derringer and fired. One damnfool mistake . . .

Sometimes one was too many.

Concentrating, he thumbed the hammer of the Colt. It moved slowly, threatening to slip. The muzzle wavered. Then suddenly the hammer heeled back, clicking as it caught at full cock.

"George, no!" Liz screamed.

She lunged — and the thunder of the gunshot echoed in the room.

She fell slowly with a strange grace, settling in a crumple of red satin. Beyond her, Glencannon saw Carlisle with the derringer in his hand. Both barrels were wisping smoke. Through clenched teeth, he said hoarsely, "That thing's empty now."

It hurt to talk. It even hurt to breathe. With his shoulders braced against the wall, he grasped the Colt in both hands trying to steady it.

Liz Gerard had taken the bullet Carlisle meant for him. Now he meant one for Carlisle. He closed his finger against the trigger. But the action felt hard. Too hard. Or else his hand was too weak.

"Drop it, Glencannon." The thin, smirking voice that came from the doorway was Shorty Steele's.

Glencannon saw Steele's lips drawn back over his teeth in a wolf-grin. Rudd Kelly's snubbed-off Greener was in the little man's hands.

Steele's face was a blur, shimmering, fading . . .

Glencannon felt the wall scraping against his shoulders. His legs were folding under him. And the sixgun was too heavy a weight for his hands. It was dragging itself out of his grip.

Fighting, he managed to close his finger on the trigger. That damned heavy trigger. At last, he felt the gun buck. But he knew it was too late. The muzzle had dropped too far. The slug plowed uselessly into the floor.

One damned mistake too many . . .

There were voices.

He couldn't be hearing voices if he were dead, could he? Glencannon asked himself the question, but he didn't feel at all certain of the answer. He thought about it in a thin, uncertain way. The thoughts seemed wispy like smoke. He couldn't hold them steady. With effort, he grabbed at them.

The pain seemed a small and distant thing. But it was growing. It became an intense throbbing in his gut.

Being dead couldn't hurt that much, he decided. And the pain pulsed as he drew breath. Dead men didn't breathe.

Convinced that he was still alive, he turned his attention to those vague voices.

". . . shot her down in cold blood, didn't he, Hartford?" That was Carlisle with his pleasantly lilting way of shaping words. He gave them a twist though, that put an edge like a threat onto them.

A voice Glencannon couldn't place asked, "Is he dead?"

He didn't recognize the one that answered either. "No. He ain't even bleeding as I can see."

They seemed to be talking about him. *Strange,* he thought abstractly. *Gunshot wounds usually bled some.* But that pain didn't feel much like any bullet he'd ever taken before. More like a mule had kicked him in the stomach.

He judged himself to be lying on a floor with one shoulder wedged against a wall. Probably still in Carlisle's office. There seemed to be a lot of people around. From the tones of the voices, he guessed that only a few minutes had passed since the shooting. He considered opening his eyes. But that would let them know he was awake. Better to get his bearings as best he could first. He lay still, listening.

"What the devil do we need Edwards

for?" That was Steele answering some comment. "If he ain't dead, he *ought* to be."

There were murmurs of agreement with the undertones of a crowd turning into a mob, building up to a lynching. Glencannon knew they were still talking about him. And that was bad. Plenty bad. Carlisle had them thinking *he* was the one who'd murdered Liz Gerard.

Something hit him in the face. Water. Grimacing against the shock of it, he opened his eyes. Shorty was standing over him, the empty glass in one hand, the Greener in the other.

With effort, Glencannon propped himself up on his elbow. Moving wasn't easy. That pain throbbed intensely in his gut.

"What happened, Glencannon?" Shorty grunted with a happy sneer. "Pass out at the sight of blood?"

What *had* happened? he asked himself. He reached his free hand to the point of the pain. His fingers found the big, thick buckle of his gunbelt. They explored the deep gouge in the metal. He remembered he'd half-turned when Carlisle fired. The derringer must have slammed its slug against the buckle, hit it at an angle and ricocheted. It had kicked the sense out of him, but it hadn't made any hole in him. Realizing that, he felt a sudden urge to laugh.

But Shorty Steele was laughing already. And there was nothing pleasant at all in the sound of it. "Hardcase, huh? Tough man, huh?" Steele mocked. "*The* Shea Glencannon, the bogeyman of Broken Crossing!" He glanced around, looking for the crowd to share his enjoyment.

"Shut up," Carlisle snapped at him.

He stopped laughing. Coldly, he ordered Glencannon to his feet. The Greener he gestured with was his authority.

Glencannon struggled himself up. Leaning against the wall, he looked past Shorty. It seemed like half the men in town must be crammed into the room, or shoving in the doorway. They stared at the body of Liz Gerard — and at him. And now that he was on his feet, evidently unhurt, the muttering grew uglier.

Shorty nudged him with the Greener, edging him toward the door. The men moved out of the way slowly. One of them hollered, "Steele, put down that damned scattergun. You pull that trigger and *he* ain't the only one who'll get peppered."

Steele shifted the shotgun, clamping it under his left arm. Unholstering a six-gun,

177

he gave it a cocky flip and ordered Glencannon down the stairs.

Moving with an awkward slowness that was only partly feigned, Glencannon took the top step. He clung to the banister hesitantly. The pain in his gut wasn't so bad now, but his vision kept blurring and his head felt packed with lint.

Shorty kept prodding at his back with the revolver. He could sense the little man's happy swagger. Well, that was just fine. It was probably the best break he'd get. He staggered down a few more steps and paused. Steele poked him with the gun again.

A few more steps and he was at the landing. As he set foot on it, he made his move.

The gun muzzle was touching his back. Twisting away, clear of it, he swung. His fist rammed into Steele's gut.

The revolver had been cocked. It went off. Glencannon could feel the sear of the muzzle flame against his back — but not the bite of lead.

Somebody somewhere on the stairs below let out a yelped curse.

Glencannon's other fist followed the first, deep into the little man's belly.

Gasping breath and muttering curses,

Steele struggled to stay on his feet. He was trying to get the gun cocked again. Glencannon's left hand wrapped around the gun. His right, fisted, aimed for Steele's face.

Steele tried to evade the blow. But as he jerked back his head, Glencannon's fist opened.

Glencannon slammed the side of his stiffened hand into the little man's Adam's apple.

Gagging, Steele half-turned as he staggered. His back was against the banister. Still wrenching at the handgun, Glencannon got a boot toe hooked under Steele's ankle. He drove for the throat again. As his hand hit, he jerked his foot.

Steele was already bent back against the railing. With a lurch, he tumbled over. And Glencannon was alone on the landing — an unobstructed target.

Somebody fired.

Glencannon felt the tug at his sleeve. Pivoting, with Steele's Colt cocked in his hand, he faced Carlisle.

The man was standing at the head of the stairs. His coat skirts were back, showing the holsters on his hips. And the pair of six-guns were in his hands. The left one was just being held handy. But the right was hammer-back and Carlisle's forefinger was closing.

Glencannon triggered the Colt.

He saw wood splinter in the wall, high and right of Carlisle's shoulder. It gave him a judgment of Steele's gun. And it startled Carlisle. He winced as his own gun spat.

The slug sang past Glencannon.

Cursing, Carlisle cocked and fired again. But Glencannon's hand was faster. He'd brought it down slightly, and leftward. He slipped the hammer.

Carlisle reeled back under the impact of lead, jerking as his own gun jumped.

With an almost studied care, Glencannon placed his third shot.

Carlisle's hand opened. The gun thudded to the floor. He fell on top of it.

Wheeling, Glencannon faced the men who'd preceded him down the stairs. But there was no challenge from them. Steele's first wild shot had clipped one man's shoulder. He crouched against the wall, hugging a hand to the wound. His lips moved in a voiceless curse and his eyes held wide on Glencannon.

The reckless lead had spooked all the rest of them. They'd scattered, spreading out through the saloon, taking cover behind overturned tables.

For the moment, their panic held them. But then it broke. Someone snapped a shot toward Glencannon. It wasn't close, but it sent him ducking back. He flattened himself against the wall.

He knew that in their own minds they had him convicted of Liz Gerard's murder. Now they meant to see him dead.

And he *couldn't* shoot it out with half the town.

Chapter 14

Cautiously Glencannon dropped to one knee. The landing was wide. As long as he crouched against the wall, it hid him from the men on the floor below. But he couldn't hide there forever. He hesitated, not sure what to do next.

"Give it up, Glencannon," somebody shouted at him. "We've got you pinned down."

That was the truth of it, he admitted to himself. If he tried to go up or down the stairs, he'd be offering himself as a target. Some one of those hotheads just might happen to be accurate with a gun. It was a chance he didn't want to take. But he didn't want to try shooting his way out either. These men weren't his enemies. There was no reason for gunplay. But how could he make them understand that?

"Glencannon, you want to *walk* down? Or be carried down?" the voice from below taunted.

Stretching out on his belly, Glencannon inched toward the edge of the landing. He could see the top of the backbar mirror. A little further and he could see the reflections of the men below in it.

Most of them were bunched up together with their backs to the mirror. They were all gazing up at the landing. Not more than half seemed to have guns. But the ones who had them were all holding them ready.

"Throw out that gun and come on down," one called.

This time he spotted the man who was doing the speaking. A broad-shouldered redhead. The same one he'd had the run-in with on the street.

"To get myself lynched?" he hollered back. "Who are you, Red? One of Carlisle's hired hands?"

"What's that supposed to mean?"

"You seem to be ramrodding this bunch. And you seem to be hellbent to get me. Maybe you got some personal reason?"

There was a faint murmuring among the men on the floor. Glencannon could tell that the talk was distracting them. He took the opportunity to examine the Colt he'd taken off Steele. There was one live round left in it. Forty-four caliber.

He cursed silently. His own gun was a

forty-five. The ammunition in his belt loops was forty-five — useless to him now.

Carlisle's guns were at the head of the stairs, he figured. Maybe he could get hold of them somehow.

He twisted around to look up — and saw the muzzle of the shotgun Steele had dropped. It lay on a step not far above. Cautiously, he snaked a hand toward it.

A slug slammed into the step in front of his face.

Snatching the Greener, he rolled. He came up onto his knees with the gun at his shoulder.

It was the redhead who'd fired that shot. He'd worked his way to the foot of the stairs. Glencannon saw him crouching half-hidden behind the heavy balustrade. It might have been good cover against the uncertain accuracy of a snap-fired hand-gun, but it was hardly protection against two barrels of a scattergun. As he saw Glencannon level the Greener toward him, he let the revolver slide out of his grip. Both hands rose, open and empty.

Glencannon gave a quick glance to the bar mirror. With their leader under the muzzle of the shotgun, none of the other men looked too eager to carry on the fight. Grinning slightly with relief, he called, "I asked you a question, Red. You ain't answered it yet."

"Huh?" The redhead stared at him in fearful bewilderment.

"Are you one of Carlisle's men?"

Red gave a slow uncertain shake of his head.

Keep talking, Glencannon told himself. *Try to argue them out of their mood. At least stall them a while longer. Edwards and the doctor'll be getting back to town eventually. They're bound to look in here. They'll lend a hand.*

He asked, "Then what are you so eager to hang me for?"

"For killing Liz Gerard!" the redhead snapped.

"You're real sure *I* shot her?"

He nodded. "Carlisle said so."

"You want to lynch me on his word?"

This time Red made no reply. He just kept staring at the shotgun in frightened confusion.

Wearily, Glencannon shifted a leg and seated himself on a step. His gut still ached. He wondered how much longer it would take for Edwards to get here. Gesturing slightly with the Greener, he said, "Suppose I decide not to fire this thing — you reckon you could restrain your enthusiasm a while? Maybe hold off your lynch party until Doc Palmer gets back and can examine the body?"

"Why?" It was an honest question. Red just plain didn't understand what Glencannon might be getting at.

"What kind of gun you think I shot Liz Gerard with?"

"Colt revolver."

"My own gun? Forty-five caliber Colt that Steele took off me?"

"Yeah," Red muttered hesitantly. He still didn't get it.

"Suppose it turned out she was killed by a forty-*one* caliber derringer. Suppose the derringer's right back where it came from, in the clip on Carlisle's arm," Glencannon suggested.

Red studied on it. He asked, "How you gonna tell what kind of gun shot her?"

"Hell, you can tell a forty-one derringer slug from a forty-five Colt one, can't you?" Glencannon hoped the redhead didn't know what could happen to a bullet if it hit bone. Mashed up, maybe shattered into pieces, one chunk of lead could look like any other piece. Even weighing them might not prove a thing.

"If she was shot with a derringer . . ." Red let his voice trail off.

Glencannon finished it for him. "If she

was shot with a derringer, then it wasn't *me* who shot her. You want to make sure of it before or after you lynch me?"

Nervously, Red looked to the men in the saloon for their opinions. Glencannon could hear the tone of their hushed, self-consciously unhappy muttering among themselves. He was satisfied with it. They'd cooled down enough to begin doubting whether they really wanted a lynch party. They'd be content to leave vengeance to the law.

"Red, you don't look any too happy standing there with your hands in the air," he said. "And I'm not very comfortable sitting here hugging this shotgun. Suppose you talk your friends into staying from behind my back, and I'll buy you a drink."

The man still looked wary and a mite spooked, but he seemed to be bucked out. He nodded.

Lowering the Greener, Glencannon got to his feet. For an instant a wave of nausea swept up from his gut. He felt himself sway dizzily. He clung to the railing until the feeling was past. Slowly, cautious of stirring it up again, he walked down the stairs.

He paused on the bottom step and looked down at Red. "What happened to Rudd Kelly?"

"He's locked in the closet. He threw that

shotgun on Steele and got it laid across his face."

"Fetch him out, will you?" Leaning over the banister, he looked at Steele. The man lay crumpled on the floor, as formless as a toppled scarecrow. "He hurt bad?"

One of the men answered, "Real bad. He's dead."

"Huh?"

"Looks like his neck is broke."

Wordlessly, Glencannon walked to one of the tables that was still upright. He put the Greener on it and slumped into a chair. There'd been too much dying.

"Shea?"

He looked up at Rudd Kelly. Except for the purpling bruise along his jaw, the bartender's face was pasty white. He dropped into a chair and gazed fully at Glencannon. "They said Liz is dead."

Tersely, Glencannon told him what had happened.

He listened the story through, then pressed his face into his hands. His shoulders jerked, but he made no sound.

Glencannon looked around for the redhead and called, "Red, why don't you bust open a couple of bottles? Drinks all around, compliments of the Glencannons."

Red hurried behind the bar and set to

work. The rest of the men crowded around him. That would hold their attention for a while, Glencannon figured.

He leaned toward Kelly and asked gently, "Where's my brother?"

Startled, Kelly looked up at him. "He — he — I don't know what you mean."

"Sure you do. It was Dale who was using my name and it was you who busted him out of jail and left a dead man in his place. What I want to know is why he was pretending to be me."

"That was Jake's idea," Kelly answered. "Dale ain't much with a gun and his name wouldn't have meant a thing. But you got yourself a reputation. Jake wanted to send for you, only he heard you were dead. He decided maybe he could pass Dale off as you and bluff Carlisle. But just your name wasn't enough to scare Carlisle. He had Steele murder Jake."

"Yeah. But why? What was it all about? Why was Liz so afraid? Why couldn't you go to the law?"

Kelly gazed toward the stairs as he struggled with his decision. Finally he muttered, "It ain't my right to tell it, but you got a right to know, and I guess I'm the only one as can tell it."

He paused, frowning. Glencannon

waited silently. After a moment, he went on. "Liz killed a man back in Omaha. He deserved it and she was right in doing it. But the law called it murder. She got away though and everything was going along fine until Carlisle showed up here. He'd known her before. He threatened to call the law down on her if she didn't pay him off."

"That's why Dale wouldn't talk when he was charged with the killing?"

"Yeah. We figured we could get him clear somehow. And as long as Carlisle thought he had a chance of cutting himself in on this business, he wouldn't spill on Liz. But if Dale went on the stand and began to talk . . ."

Glencannon nodded. "Can Dale prove he didn't kill Pa?"

"We figured he could, only we couldn't take a chance — not with Carlisle threatening Liz."

"Liz is dead now. So's Carlisle. Dale's going to have to come back and get it all straightened out."

"Why?" Kelly asked. "Ain't it all right now?"

"Ted knows the man he had in jail as me ain't dead. He'll set out looking for that man and he's already got the law hunting

190

for my brother. Those two trails will come together for sure. Better if Dale comes in and squares it away first."

"Yeah," the barkeep muttered.

"And I got to square myself of Liz's murder."

"Huh?"

"Yeah. Carlisle told the crowd I'd done it and they believed him. I barely managed to talk myself out of a quick lynching," Glencannon said. That was one time he'd been able to work something out with words instead of having to fight it out. J.J.'d have been proud of him, he thought.

J.J.'d had the knack for that sort of thing. He'd been able to turn men's minds this way and that with his talking. Remembering, Glencannon told himself that J.J. would have been able to talk Harry Wolfe right into a lawful noose if only he'd been able to get to the governor. But J.J. couldn't do any more talking now and the damned witnesses wouldn't even try . . .

"Witnesses!" he said aloud.

"What?" Kelly grunted.

"I got a witness," Glencannon told him. "That lawyer, Hartford. He saw it all, only Carlisle had him cowed. You reckon now that Carlisle's dead, he'll tell the truth?"

"As lawyers go, he's honest enough,"

Kelly answered. "Most likely he —"

"Horses coming," somebody hollered.

Wrapping a hand around the Greener, Glencannon headed for the door. Outside, Edwards and Palmer were stepping down off their horses. Scowling at the shotgun, Edwards grunted, "What's been going on here?"

"Where's Christy?" Glencannon asked.

Palmer came up to him. "We left her at my place. My housekeeper and the Grady girl are looking after her. She's all right. But you don't look so good."

"I got kicked in the stomach."

"What's happened here?" Edwards repeated.

The men bunched around listening as Glencannon told him the whole of it. They muttered among themselves but no one denied that it had happened the way Glencannon said.

When he was done, Edwards held a hand toward him. "I'd better take that shotgun."

"Here." Glencannon gave it to him, then turned and started up the walk.

"Shea!" the marshal called. "There's still that Gwinnett business. . . ."

Glencannon looked back over his shoulder. "Go to hell."

"Shea, you gave me your parole."

A lawman clear through the bone, Glencannon thought with a touch of admiration. Ted and J.J. would have got along real fine together. Only J.J. was dead now. So many people dead. He was sick of death.

Slowly, he said, "I'm too damned tired, Ted. I'm going to bed. If you want to arrest me again, see me in the morning."

Chapter 15

The sun was high beyond the small window. It made a bright square of light on the rumpled bedclothes. Glencannon yawned. Propping his head on his hands, he gazed at the clear blue of the sky. It was going to be another hot, dust-laden day. Didn't it ever rain in Broken Crossing any more?

For a long while he just lay there going over his thoughts. He felt no satisfaction at the decision he came to. He wasn't at all sure it would work. And there was one more question to be asked. Until he knew the answer to that, he couldn't be certain about the plan.

He took his time getting dressed and stowing his loose gear in the saddlebags. It wouldn't be an easy question to ask. He wasn't handy with words the way J.J. had been. Finally he slung the saddlebags over his shoulder and headed downstairs.

Edwards was waiting in the lobby. As he spotted Glencannon he jumped out of his chair and hurried over. But before he could speak, Glencannon asked him sharply, "Christy still at Doc Palmer's?"

He nodded.

"And Sherry?"

"Yeah. Look, Shea . . ."

Glencannon turned away from him and strode toward the street door. He rushed to catch up. As he came alongside, Glencannon asked him, "You still figure on arresting me, Ted?"

"I still got that telegram from Harry Wolfe."

"Got it with you?"

He fingered at his pocket and brought out the folded slip of paper.

"Good," Glencannon grunted.

Eyeing the saddlebags, Edwards asked, "Shea, where you think you're going?"

"Doc Palmer's."

The marshal had a feeling he wasn't going to get any explanation unless he tagged along. He followed Glencannon to the doctor's house. At the door, Glencannon rapped, then turned to face him.

"Ted, it might be I'm wrong. If I am, it's me that'll end up dead this time. But I got to do this my way."

The door swung open. Palmer stood there in his shirtsleeves. Grinning sociably, he said, "Come on in. The coffee's still hot."

He led them into the kitchen. Christy Gerard and Sherry Grady were both there, seated at the breakfast table.

"Shea!" Christy jumped up and ran toward him, grabbing his hand.

Palmer found two more cups and filled them. He handed them out. With a glance at the saddlebags, he asked Glencannon, "Leaving?"

"Yeah."

There was disappointment in Christy's face. Hopefully, she asked, "Will you come back?"

"I'm planning to. Soon as I get some business settled."

"What business, Shea?" Edwards put in. "Where you figure on going?"

Glencannon looked at the marshal, but his attention was on Sherry Grady. "Gwinnett. I kinda left a job half-done back there."

"Harry will kill you," Sherry said. He couldn't read the meaning in her voice. Was it a threat — or a warning?

"I don't like the idea of a murder warrant against me," he told her. "I figure I better stand trial and get myself cleared. If I go back by way of Tucson, I can have a talk with the governor, the way J.J. was planning to do. And when I ride into Gwinnett, maybe I'll have the governor or some of his friends along with me. I think if I shake that town hard enough, some of those scared-rabbit witnesses will come out of their holes. If I go at it right, maybe I can bust Harry Wolfe and his crowd. Finish up the job J.J. set out to do."

J.J. could have made it work, he thought. He wasn't so sure about himself. Could he win a fight with words instead of guns? Facing Sherry, he said, "You want to ride along with me?"

She just stared at him, dumbfounded by the question.

"You got to go back, you know," he said slowly. "You have to be there if they're going to try me for shooting Charlie."

Her eyes were bewildered. He turned away, feeling that he was doing this all wrong somehow. But he kept on talking. "You know, if *you* were to go to Tucson with me and talk to the governor — if you were to stand up in front of a judge and jury and speak out everything you know about Harry Wolfe and his crowd, *you* could bust him. It wouldn't do Charlie any good now, but — look, Sherry, maybe it was me that shot Charlie but it was Harry who *murdered* him. Can't you see that? If you stand up and speak against Harry, you can bust him. You can stop him from making killers out of more boys like Charlie. If getting me hanged is worth more to you than that —"

He cut himself short, feeling frustrated and embarrassed. The words had gotten tangled up between his thinking them and his saying them. If he couldn't convince one lone woman, how the hell could he expect to convince the territorial governor, the judge and the jury?

He took a sip of the coffee, then turned to Palmer. "Doc, will you look after Christy? Kind of take care of her and the business until my brother gets here and can take over?"

"Of course." The doctor smiled.

"You will come back?" Christy asked again. She was still clinging to his hand.

"Sure." He grinned at her as he shook free of her grip. Then he turned to Edwards. "Can I have that telegram to take along?"

The marshal handed it to him. As he pocketed it, he told himself that at least Edwards was convinced. Maybe he was hoping for too much when he asked Sherry to believe him and help him.

He shifted the saddlebag, resettling it on his shoulder, and realized he was stalling. He didn't want to leave yet. Not with things still like this. But he knew he didn't have anything else left to say to Sherry. Reluctantly, he started toward the door.

"Glencannon!"

He looked back over his shoulder.

Sherry'd risen to her feet. The expression in her face was strange. Her voice was hesitant. "I — I'll go to Tucson with you."

A feeling of relief flooded through him. The doubts were all gone. Words had worked with her. They'd work in Gwinnett, too. He'd finish the job — finish it the way J.J. would have done.

Sherry's eyes were searching and uncertain. But there was no look of hatred for him in them. He looked back at her. Grinning slightly, he told himself that maybe, in time, he could work out everything.

The employees of Thorndike Press hope you have enjoyed this Large Print book. All our Thorndike and Wheeler Large Print titles are designed for easy reading, and all our books are made to last. Other Thorndike Press Large Print books are available at your library, through selected bookstores, or directly from us.

For information about titles, please call:

(800) 223-1244

or visit our Web site at:

www.gale.com/thorndike
www.gale.com/wheeler

To share your comments, please write:

Publisher
Thorndike Press
295 Kennedy Memorial Drive
Waterville, ME   04901

4